HOME on the RANCH

HOME *on the* **RANCH**

ROPING
THE RANCHER

— ✠ —

JULIE
BENSON

 HARLEQUIN® HOME ON THE RANCH

Recycling programs
for this product may
not exist in your area.

ISBN-13: 978-1-335-45337-2

Roping the Rancher

Copyright © 2014 by Julie Benson

All rights reserved. Except for use in any review, the reproduction or utilization of this work in whole or in part in any form by any electronic, mechanical or other means, now known or hereafter invented, including xerography, photocopying and recording, or in any information storage or retrieval system, is forbidden without the written permission of the publisher, Harlequin Enterprises Limited, 22 Adelaide St. West, 40th Floor, Toronto, Ontario M5H 4E3, Canada.

This is a work of fiction. Names, characters, places and incidents are either the product of the author's imagination or are used fictitiously, and any resemblance to actual persons, living or dead, business establishments, events or locales is entirely coincidental.

This edition published by arrangement with Harlequin Books S.A.

For questions and comments about the quality of this book, please contact us at CustomerService@Harlequin.com.

® and TM are trademarks of Harlequin Enterprises Limited or its corporate affiliates. Trademarks indicated with ® are registered in the United States Patent and Trademark Office, the Canadian Intellectual Property Office and in other countries.

Printed in U.S.A.

An avid daydreamer since childhood, **Julie Benson** always loved creating stories. After graduating from the University of Texas at Dallas with a degree in sociology, she worked as case manager before having her children: three boys. Many years later she started pursuing a writing career to challenge her mind and save her sanity. Now she writes full-time in Dallas, where she lives with her husband, their sons, two lovable black dogs, two guinea pigs, a turtle and a fish. When she finds a little quiet time, which isn't often, she enjoys making jewelry and reading a good book.

For Sue Casteel
and the other volunteers and staff at Equest
Therapeutic Horsemanship in Wylie, Texas, without
whom this book couldn't have been written. The
amazing work you do changes lives for the better.

Chapter 1

"I don't care how good the therapy is supposed to be. There is no way I'm letting you get on a horse," Stacy Michaels said to her younger brother when they left his neurologist's office.

"This isn't about me. It's about Dad, isn't it?"

"Of course it is." Stacy punched the elevator down button with so much force she chipped her fingernail.

"Dad died filming a movie stunt. This is a therapy program," Ryan insisted.

Since he'd been only a few months old at the time, he knew nothing about their father's death other than what he'd been told.

While an eleven-year-old Stacy had been in the movie as well and witnessed the entire event. Even now, almost sixteen years later, some nights she still woke drenched in sweat from the nightmares.

The months before her dad's accident had been the best time in Stacy's life. She smiled at the memories of working with him on the movie and how she soaked up every drop of attention he poured on her. The image of him beaming when he told everyone within earshot how she was a chip off the old block and that one day she'd be a star flashed in her mind.

Her life had been perfect.

Then a week before filming ended, her father, playing a fifteenth-century knight, was shooting the big battle scene against her character's kidnappers. When his mount became spooked by the special effects, her father fell and the horse trampled him to death, with Stacy a few feet away.

Now her brother wanted her to give the okay for him to become a patient of a therapeutic horse program. Not as long as she was his guardian.

"There has to be another option."

"You heard what Dr. Chapman said. We've tried everything else. This is my best shot to walk without this damned walker," Ryan said, as he struggled to maneuver onto the elevator.

A year ago Ryan had been driving when a man walked out onto the street from between two parked cars. Unable to avoid the man, Ryan hit him and then barreled head-on into a telephone phone pole. The man nearly died. Both of Ryan's legs were crushed and he'd sustained a brain injury that left him with control and balance issues. Despite two surgeries and countless hours of physical therapy, he still needed a walker. The investigation cleared Ryan of any wrongdoing, but he'd still carried a fair share of guilt over what happened.

Stacy stared at her brother, his eyes filled with determination and, more importantly, hope. Her breath caught in her throat. She hadn't seen that emotion in his gaze for months. He deserved every chance to get his life back to what it had been, but how could she let him get on a horse? "I don't know."

"Please, you've got to let me try this. Whatever the risk, for me it's worth it."

She told herself he wouldn't be racing around hell-for-leather on a movie set with cannons booming around him like their father had been. From what Dr. Chapman said, the horse Ryan rode for therapy would be walking or at most trotting around an arena with multiple volunteers to ensure nothing went wrong. She glanced at her brother. He was so young. How could she deny him this chance to get his life back? "You win."

"You're the best."

"And don't you forget it."

Once in the car Ryan stuck his nose in the program brochures the doctor had given them, occasionally tossing out information. "Most of the programs have spring sessions starting this time of year. That means I can start right away. In ten weeks I could be ditching my walker."

"Where's the closest one?" Stacy asked, her mind starting to work on how she'd carve time out of her schedule to accommodate his therapy sessions.

Then a thought hit her. Her next movie, *The Women of Spring Creek Ranch,* was scheduled to start shooting next week in Estes Park, Colorado.

Unless she figured out a way to be in two places at once, she had a problem.

"Mom, Ryan had another appointment with the neurologist this afternoon. You told me you'd be there." Stacy fought to keep her voice level despite her growing irritation as she walked into the living room of her mother's recently redecorated Malibu beach house.

"I went out to lunch with some friends and lost track of time."

More likely she lost track of how many cosmos she'd had, and based on her bleary-eyed gaze, smeared mascara and rumpled blouse and slacks, she had passed out the minute she got home.

Which was exactly why Ryan had asked Stacy to sue for guardianship. They'd both hoped Andrea losing custody of her son would be the wake-up call she needed to pull herself together. So far that hadn't been the case.

"I know I should've been there, but I've had so many doctor appointments of my own." Andrea, a passenger in the car with Ryan, had broken her arm. She'd also received minor cuts to her face and neck, for which she'd insisted on plastic surgery to repair. She'd also attended biweekly sessions with her therapist to cope with the emotional trauma. "I couldn't bear facing another doctor. Plus, you're so much better dealing with Ryan's problems than I am."

Same old story. Her mom couldn't cope so she bailed on her son.

Stacy sank onto the couch beside her mother,

took a deep breath and recounted the details from Ryan's doctor appointment.

"I don't know if that's a good idea considering what happened to your father." Andrea's voice broke. "I still miss him so much. How could God have taken him when he always took care of me?"

The accident that killed Stacy's father was the first blow that sent Andrea's world spinning. Her mother had taken to her bed. If it hadn't been for their nanny, Stacy didn't know what would've happened to her and Ryan. Molly had been the one she clung to when she woke from nightmares. When she skinned her knee, she ran to Molly who hugged her and dried her tears.

Stacy's life changed even more when the movie she filmed with her father opened a year later. Critics raved not only about Jason Michaels's performance, but Stacy's, as well. Talk shows wanted to interview her. Directors sent scripts to her father's agent for consideration. The next thing Stacy knew, she had a full-time job.

Her focus changed from studying for her weekly spelling test to preparing for her next audition. Six months later she landed a role on what turned out to be an Emmy-award-winning series, *The Kids Run the Place,* that ran for ten years. Looking back now, she realized being on that show saved her life. The cast became more of a family than her own had ever been. She'd often pretended her TV parents were her real parents. One day she even begged Sophia Granger, her TV mom, to take her home with her.

Don't think about that now. Concentrate on Ryan's problem, and getting Mom to see he needs her.

"The doctor thinks the therapeutic sports riding will improve Ryan's muscle control and balance," Stacy said, summarizing the information she'd read on the internet. The horse's rhythmic movement was what helped people. To control and direct the horse the patient had to master his own body. The skills learned on horseback then carried over into the patient's everyday life. "The risk of something going wrong is minuscule." Maybe if she said the words enough she'd believe them, too. "Ryan wants this chance at a normal life."

"I trust you to decide what's best. I don't know what I'd do without you to take care of things."

Maybe you'd have to face reality for a change and be the parent.

Resisting the urge to massage her aching temples, Stacy counted to ten, trying to dredge up more patience, because all she wanted to do was shake her mother and scream for her to snap out of it. Not that doing so would do any good. Her mother would only burst into tears and ask how her daughter could say that to her when she was still dealing with the pain caused by her injuries and her recent separation from husband number three.

Grant had turned out to be prime marriage material. Three months ago he claimed his wife's physical and emotional problems from the car accident were draining him creatively, and the negative energy was affecting his auditions, costing him roles. Then he moved out.

"I start filming next week. I was hoping you could go with Ryan to therapy."

Stacy reached into her purse, pulled out the list of programs and held the paper out to her mother. "The doctor highlighted the ones he thought were the best."

Her mother scanned the information. "These are all out of town. I can't go anywhere. Grant and I are meeting tomorrow to talk about reconciling." Her mother's blue eyes sparkled, as she toyed with a strand of golden hair, highlighted perfectly and often to cover the gray. "He says he misses me. That his life is so empty without me."

Stacy wanted to laugh at her mother's naïveté. More likely Grant missed his bills being paid and the lifestyle he'd become accustomed to living with Andrea. Life had to be less pleasant for him when he had to actually earn a living.

"That's wonderful that he's willing to talk about a reconciliation, but Ryan needs—"

"I still can't believe Grant moved out." Tears pooled in Andrea's eyes. "I thought we'd be together forever. That he'd take care of me."

Maybe you should learn to take care of yourself. That way you wouldn't end up devastated when a man lets you down.

The biting words sat perched on Stacy's tongue. While it would feel cathartic to confront her mom, dealing with the emotional meltdown afterward wasn't worth it.

Andrea glanced at the therapy information again. "It says here therapy is once a week. Couldn't you hop on a quick flight, go to therapy with Ryan and then fly right back to the set?"

Stacy swallowed hard. She wouldn't be here banging her head against the wall trying to get Andrea to help out if the problem were that easily fixed. "I can't be gone for an entire day every week."

Her mom frowned and crossed her arms over her chest. "I certainly can't be locked into weekly appointments. I have to be here to work on my marriage. That and healing physically from the accident have to be my top priorities."

"This is exactly why Ryan doesn't think you care about him."

"That's not fair. I love my son. I just need to concentrate on myself right now. That's what my therapist says. Until I do that I don't have anything to give to anyone else."

Life had dealt her mother some tough hits, but that didn't give her the right to crawl in her shell and forget about her son.

"I need to do this movie. Finances are tight."

Andrea waived a delicate manicured hand through the air. "You're just like your father, always worrying about money. He was always a sky is falling type, too."

Stacy sighed, and clasped her hands on her lap. Andrea received a generous settlement when Stacy's father died, but she lived as though the money would never run out. How many times would they have to go over budget basics before her mother understood? Apparently at least once more. "Your expenses have to be less than your income. Since your divorce from Allan, that hasn't been the case. We had to liquidate a lot of your investments in the divorce settlement."

Her mother bit her lip. For a second she looked older than her years, and Stacy's heart tightened. "I wish I'd listened to you about asking him to sign a prenup. I was just so scared that if I did he'd say I didn't trust him, and he'd leave me."

Which he did anyway. While a broken engagement would've been tough on her mother, it would have been less financially painful than a messy divorce. Why couldn't her mother see that?

Because she's so desperate for love.

"Mom, you have to stick to the budget we made out. You can't just disregard—"

"Don't start lecturing me about how I spent too much money redecorating the house before Grant and I got married." Andrea folded her hands, which were still young-looking, thanks to weekly deep moisturizing treatments, on her lap. "I don't regret spending a penny of that money. I wanted him to feel like this was his house. Part of the reason my marriage with Allan failed was he felt like he was living in your father's shadow."

"I'm trying to explain why you need to make some changes. If insurance pays for

Ryan's therapy at all, it'll reimburse us. I can't afford to lose out on work right now."

Especially when I'm the only working member of the family, and it's been a while since I had a hit movie or series.

Her mother frowned. Tears filled her eyes again. "I'm sorry we've been such a burden to you."

No. Andrea's "poor me" routine wouldn't work today. She refused to feel guilty. This was all about Ryan and what he needed. "We're a family, and family helps each other out."

But shouldn't the flow go both ways?

"Grant and I might still be able to make our marriage work." Her mother's lips trembled, and her voice broke. "I don't know if I can survive another divorce. Stacy, you have to help me. You've got to give me this chance. Can't you see if they can work the shooting schedule around Ryan's therapy?"

"I was lucky to get this role. Half of the actresses in Hollywood wanted it."

"Nonsense. That woman owes you," her mother said, a sneer on her face as she referred to Maggie Sullivan McAlister, the creator and director of *The Women of Spring Creek Ranch*.

"No one gave me the part. I *earned* it."

"After what she did on that dreadful reality dating show, she's lucky you didn't sue her for every penny she had. I still can't believe that cowboy chose the plain Jane director over you."

Stacy only agreed to be a bachelorette on *Finding Mrs. Right* because she'd been between jobs. Never once had she considered letting her heart get involved with the bachelor. She hadn't been foolish enough to believe a reality show relationship would last longer than the latest fashion fad. For her, the show had been a job like any other TV show. A vehicle to getting a series of her own.

"I got over that ages ago." Now if only other people would quit bringing the subject up, she could forget about it, too. "If I ask Maggie to shoot around Ryan's therapy I risk her giving the role to someone else. Mom, please go with Ryan so I can do this movie."

There, she'd put it all on the line. She told her mother exactly what she needed. Stacy held her breath, and prayed this once her mother would pull up her mom panties and be the parent.

"Grant and I need time to work out our problems. Then I can go with Ryan for therapy. Surely waiting a month or two won't make that much difference."

So much for Andrea stepping up and doing the right thing by putting her children first.

"He shouldn't have to wait until it's convenient for us." Ryan deserved this chance, and apparently she was the only one willing to make it happen.

As a child, whenever she asked her mom to play a game or read a book to her, the response had always been, "In a minute." Or, "Not now." Or, "Ask the nanny." That taught Stacy a valuable lesson. Asking for something led to disappointment. When she learned to quit asking, she avoided that pain.

Harnessing her anger, Stacy mumbled something about how she'd take care of Ryan's therapy, said goodbye to Andrea and stumbled out of the house. Once inside her car, she dropped her head to the steering wheel and cried.

A minute later Stacy dried her tears and told herself to snap out of it. A pity party never helped. All it did was wreck a girl's makeup, and leave her with red, puffy eyes. There had to be a solution. All she had to do was find it.

Later that afternoon as Stacy sat in her cozy Hollywood condo, she faced the truth. She could either do the movie or she could give her brother a chance to recover.

There would always be another movie. Maybe not as wonderful a role as the lead in *The Women of Spring Creek Ranch,* but losing the job wouldn't kill her career. Of course she'd have to solve her cash-flow problem. She'd call her agent and ask him to get her any work he could find to bring in some quick money without requiring a long commitment. Commercials. Voice-over work, whatever, as long as the job paid. Her career would be fine.

Provided Maggie understood. Otherwise Stacy could find herself blacklisted with every director in town. Her hand shook as she picked up her cell phone. "Maggie, I hate to do this, but I've got to drop out of the movie. My brother needs physical therapy. It's a ten-week program, and right now I need to be with him. I can't be on location for a movie and get him to his therapy sessions."

"While I'm disappointed we won't get to work together, I understand. Family has to come first."

Such a simple concept. How come her mother couldn't grasp it? "The doctor says his best chance to walk again is a therapeutic horse program."

"That's the therapy where patients ride horses, isn't it?"

"It is."

"One of the things about a small town is anything happens and everyone knows about it," Maggie said. "You're not going to believe this, but Colt Montgomery, a war vet, opened a program like that on his ranch a while ago. It's a couple miles down the road from where we'll be filming at Twin Creeks."

The image of the stereotypical crotchety rancher in the old Westerns popped into Stacy's mind. The one who preferred his horse's company to people. Who cared if it was Rooster Cogburn running the program if he helped Ryan?

"The program's new, and I don't know anything about it," Maggie continued, "but if it's an option for your brother, you might be able to arrange his therapy around our shooting schedule."

Who would've thought she and Stacy would work together after how things had gone between them on the reality show *Finding Mrs. Right?* Stacy bit her lip, trying to control her emotions at Maggie's unexpected kindness. Her mother wouldn't help, but here was someone, barely an acquaintance, who was willing to do what she could to alleviate her problem. Tears blurred her vision. "You'd do that?"

"You could pop over to the Rocking M

Ranch for a therapy session during your downtime. If your brother's doctor thinks the program will work, I'm willing to give it a try. The name of Colt's program is Healing Horses."

"Maggie, I can't tell you how much I appreciate this, especially considering what I said to you and Griffin during the finale."

Stacy had been one of the bachelorettes on the show competing for the heart of a Colorado cowboy, Griffin McAlister. Because of that opportunity she'd received a deal for her own reality show. However, things had been contingent on her getting a marriage proposal and the free publicity that went along with the engagement ring as the "winner" of *Finding Mrs. Right*. Never one to leave situations to chance and sensing Griffin was as enthusiastic about marital bliss as she was, Stacy approached him with a deal. He'd propose. They'd play the happy couple during the post-show appearances, and then quietly break up. She'd say they parted amicably, and he'd do likewise. They'd fulfill their contracts, get the free publicity to help their careers and come out without a scratch to their images. A win-win situation all around.

But things hadn't gone as planned. Instead, Griffin and Maggie fell in love and he proposed to the director instead during the live finale. At the time all Stacy saw was her latest career opportunity flying out the window and she'd been brutal in her anger.

"I owe you an apology, too," Maggie said. "I couldn't talk to you at the audition with everyone else around, but I want to tell you that now. I know people say 'we didn't plan this, it just happened' all the time, but that really was the case with me and Griffin. The more we worked together, the more we got to know each other, and we fell in love."

"I think you were the only one who got to see the real man," Stacy said. When she was with Griffin on a date she'd sensed he was holding back, that he was treating the show like a job, too. Looking back now she saw that fact even more. He hadn't been shocked by her business proposition. His only concern had been whether he could trust her to keep quiet about their deal. Once she'd answered that question, he'd agreed. In fact he'd appeared almost relieved, but then he'd pulled the rug out from under her at the finale.

"I'm hoping Healing Horses will work for Ryan because I'd love to work with you. I think this project is going to be amazing."

As she told Maggie she'd talk to Ryan's doctor and call her no later than tomorrow with an answer, hope and determination blossomed inside of Stacy.

With a little luck Ryan would get his therapy and she could make the movie. Another win-win situation. Hopefully this one would work out better than the last one.

Chapter 2

Boring. Calm. Uneventful. Ordinary. The words once made Colt Montgomery go stir-crazy, but since coming home from Afghanistan, they sounded pretty damned good. Of course, raising a teenage daughter on his own meant he didn't use those words in conjunction with his life very often, but he kept hoping.

Everywhere he went in town people and life seemed the same, and yet he wasn't. Life in Afghanistan consisted of endless monotony and preparation, interrupted with bouts of sheer terror. He spent a good portion of his day wondering if someone he was there to help would turn on him with an AK-47. Then one day he was home.

Going to a war zone changed a man in ways few could understand, but he was one of the lucky ones. He'd come home with all his body parts. Except for some minor scars and an occasional nightmare, he returned unscathed, but then he hadn't been there for his full tour, either.

Once home, he struggled with what to do with his life. While he loved being a parent, he needed more than raising his daughter and being a rancher. Then he heard from one of his buddies, Dan, who'd lost a leg in Afghanistan. His doctor recommended an equestrian sports therapy program, but there wasn't one near him. After that email, Colt discovered the purpose he craved in creating Healing Horses.

He'd gone through a seven-week training course to become a registered instructor. Then he started training horses and found local physical therapists willing to donate their time to recommend activities and work with clients when necessary.

When Colt finally was able to open the doors to Healing Horses, Dan was the program's first patient.

Footsteps tapped across the wooden floor outside his office. He looked up from the stack of bills due on his desk to see his daughter walk in, and his heart ached.

He'd come so close to losing her when he was in Afghanistan, and all because of his selfishness. When her mother ran off with a computer repairman and died a month later in a car accident, he should've quit the National Guard Reserves. He'd known getting deployed was a possibility, but he never really thought it would happen. So much for long shots.

When he'd been shipped to Afghanistan, his younger brother came to Colorado to stay with Jess. Reed, a bachelor, made more than a few mistakes, and Jess ran away. What could have happened to her, now that gave Colt real nightmares. Pimps. Drug dealers. General crazies waiting to prey on a naive fourteen-year-old. He thanked God every day that Reed and Avery, now Reed's wife, found Jess at the Denver airport before she got into any serious trouble.

Jess's running away had been a hard kick to the head for Colt. This time he got the message. She was the most important thing in his life and it was high time he proved it. So he asked for a hardship discharge, left the National Guard Reserves and returned to Estes Park.

Looking at her now standing in his office,

he realized every day she looked more like her mother. Same petite frame, long chestnut hair and warm coffee-colored eyes as her mother. Jess was the constant reminder of how young and in love he'd once been. Sometimes he looked at her and tried to find bits of himself. Today he didn't have any trouble finding a similarity. Her chin pointed at him in stubborn defiance she inherited from him. He braced himself for whatever hand grenade she was about to throw his way.

"Cody Simmons asked me out to a movie on Saturday. Can I go?"

He closed his eyes for a second to regroup. Times like these he missed having her mother around to tell him whether or not he was being too much of a hard-ass. "As in out for a date, asked you out?"

"The word *date* was never mentioned."

"I'm not falling for that one again." She'd burned him with technicalities more than once before he learned to choose his words very carefully and scrutinize every one of hers for land mines. "Would you be going with a group of friends?"

"Not exactly, but—"

"Then it's a date, and the answer is no."

Cody was a good kid. He was an honor student, worked part-time at the Cinemaplex and was a pretty good bronc rider in the junior rodeo circuit, but none of that mattered to Colt. Just thinking about Jess dating shoved his panic into overdrive, especially since he knew what seventeen-year-old boys were like. Basically a bundle of hormones fantasizing about sex every thirty seconds. He hadn't been much older than Cody when he and Lynn started having sex. By graduation she'd been pregnant and they were planning a quickie wedding.

No way did he want history repeating itself with his daughter.

"Your 'no dating until I'm sixteen' rule is so old-fashioned."

"Then you better go get your bonnet, missy."

Three more months were all he had before he started greeting boys at the door with a shotgun and giving them his own version of the Spanish Inquisition before he let them out the door with his daughter. He now understood why man invented the chastity belt.

"All my friends have been dating since they were fifteen. What difference will a few months make?"

"What difference will it make to wait?"

She crossed her arms over her chest, shifted her weight onto one foot and glared at him. Such determination and strength, and yet so much hurt behind those beautiful brown eyes. How could a mother walk out on such a wonderful child?

Leaving him, he got. He and Lynn had troubles from the moment the ink dried on their marriage license. She wanted so much that he couldn't give her. Bright lights, the big city, adventure. Being a military wife and later a rancher's wife weren't what she had in mind.

If only he'd known that earlier, but they'd been high-school sweethearts who swore the love they felt would last forever. They were too young and foolish to know what they didn't know. He wondered now if their relationship would've run its course sooner if Lynn hadn't gotten pregnant.

But then he wouldn't have Jess, and he wouldn't trade being her father for anything. She was the only good thing that came out of his marriage.

"You don't understand what it's like being the only one who can't date. I'll become a social outcast."

He bit his lip to keep from laughing at her woeful my-life-is-over look and drama queen voice. To a teenage girl everything turned into a Greek tragedy. Life with her was like walking a tightrope. One misstep, either with being too strict or too permissive, could lead to a big fall.

"In a couple of days everyone will forget that your hard-ass dad won't let you date."

"If I say no, Cody will probably ask another girl to go with him."

Good. All the better.

Instead, Colt said, "If he really likes you, he'll wait until you turn sixteen."

"Guys have needs—"

"What the hell do you know about that?"

His blood pressure approaching stroke levels, he prayed his daughter wasn't talking about the kind of needs he knew about all too well. His ate him up so bad sometimes he couldn't sleep at night. Hell, he couldn't remember the last time he'd gotten laid. Sure he'd taken the edge off, but that wasn't the same as being with a woman. Sometimes holding one, losing himself in her warm curves and pretending they cared about each other was the only thing that would ease the ache.

For about five minutes when he'd first returned from Afghanistan, he considered dating. Then he remembered what it was like living in the small town he grew up in where gossiping was a town sport. The last thing he wanted was people talking about his love life and his teenage daughter hearing the stories.

On top of that, a casual relationship, in a lot of ways, sounded worse to him than no relationship at all, but he refused to have any other kind. One disastrous marriage was enough.

"Guys have fragile egos," Jess said, easing his panic somewhat. "Getting turned down for a date is hard on their self-esteem. He'll find someone who can go out with him."

"She's not my concern."

"I know. I am."

"That's right."

"Just because you don't have a life, doesn't mean I can't have one."

Ouch. He'd died and gone to hell, and this conversation was his punishment. "I've got a life."

But her words got him thinking. What did he have other than Jess? A brother and sister-in-law. The ranch he grew up on. His therapy program, Healing Horses. Was that enough? It had to be right now. He couldn't handle anything else. Definitely not dating and the emotional pitfalls that went along with trying to maintain a romantic relationship. Life with a teenager was exhausting enough.

"A monk has a more exciting life than you

do," his daughter said. "You've got work. That's not the same. What're you going to do when I go to college in two years? I don't want you to end up being one of those weird old men who lives alone and talks to himself all day long."

Apparently he hadn't been the only one wondering what his life would be like when Jess went off to college. Part of him dreaded her leaving, while a piece of him looked forward to the freedom he'd have. For as long as he could remember responsibilities ruled his life. From the time he and Reed were strong enough to lift a saddle his father had worked his sons harder than any ranch hand. As the big brother, he'd watched out for Reed. Colt had stepped in to defuse things once their mother, the family peacemaker and punching bag, died. Then at eighteen he'd found himself in the military responsible for a wife with a baby on the way.

An empty nest and the chance to figure out what he wanted to do with the rest of his life sounded pretty good right now.

"Your life shouldn't stop because you've got me to raise."

"It hasn't." He picked up the top bill and scanned the paper, hoping his daughter would take the hint that he was done discussing her dating and his.

"Why don't you trust me?" Jess accused. "I thought you'd forgiven me for running away."

Jess's quiet words and the clear pain in her expressive brown eyes hit Colt hard like a kick from an angry mule. He replaced the bill on the stack. "I have. I know if you're ever that upset again, you'll come to me, and we'll work things out. I don't want you to ever be afraid to tell me anything."

Unlike how he and Reed had been with their father, who they tried every trick to avoid. The old man was as likely to greet a simple good morning from his sons with a slap upside the head as a smile, and there was never a way to predict which they'd get or change the outcome. "I trust you. It's the boys that scare the hell out of me."

"We'd just being going to a movie."

He'd told himself he wouldn't be the hard liner his father had been. He wouldn't drive his daughter away. The last thing he wanted her thinking was that he didn't trust her. He sighed. Time to cowboy up and prove the fact. "I'll compromise. Make it a double date, and you can go."

His daughter charged around his desk, flung her arms around him and squeezed him tight. "I won't let you down," she whispered in his ear and kissed him on the cheek. Then with one last grin, she headed for the door as Nannette McAlister, his assistant at Healing Horses, strolled in. "You'll never guess what happened. Dad said I could go out on a double date this Friday."

"You finally wore him down, huh?" Nannette was the kind of mother every child should have. She loved and encouraged her three children, and their friends were always welcome in the McAlister home. All she wanted was for them to be happy. His brother had found that out firsthand.

Since Reed married Avery, Nannette's youngest and only daughter, he and Jess had been enveloped in the family fold, as well.

"I'm putting my full trust in my daughter," Colt said to Nannette to emphasize his point with Jess. "She promised she won't let me down."

Jess shook her head. "I'm leaving before he changes his mind."

"Smart girl."

"I take after my father," Jess said before she dashed off.

"How's the morning going?" Nannette asked once she'd settled at her desk, and started booting up her computer.

"Better now that Jess is gone. This dating stuff is going to kill me."

The older woman smiled knowingly. "I feel your pain. Raising Avery gave me more gray hairs than her brothers combined. I know it doesn't seem like it sometimes, but you will survive having a teenage daughter."

"Thank goodness you keep reminding me of that."

When Nannette heard about him turning the Rocking M into a horse-therapy ranch, she'd immediately volunteered to help with bookkeeping. Then when they started classes, she'd assumed scheduling duties, as well. Taking the money he'd gotten from the grant Healing Horses received three months ago to hire Nannette McAlister had been the smartest thing he'd ever done.

When her computer finished booting up, she punched some keys and said, "We received another client application." The hum of the printer filled the office. Nannette grabbed the paper, scanned the application and froze. "This can't be the same Stacy Michaels."

"I need a little context, Nannette. So far you aren't making a lot of sense."

She walked across the room and handed him the paper. "Stacy Michaels was one of the finalists when Griffin was on that ridiculous dating show."

Colt had wondered what kind of woman went on a show like that and fought with a pack of women to win the "love" of a man they'd just met.

A woman whose moral compass didn't point due north, that's who.

From the little bit he saw of the show, he remembered flighty, beautiful women with long legs and short form-fitting skirts that almost showed the good china. Great to look at, but no substance. Women who'd looked down their more-often-than-not surgically altered noses at just about everyone.

After glancing at the application, he said, "It doesn't matter if it's the same woman or not because she wants to sign her brother up for the spring therapeutic sports riding session. It's already started and it's full." He picked up his phone and punched in the number listed on the application. The sultry feminine voice that answered could get a rise out of a man two months after he was dead and buried. His pulse rate shot up like a rodeo bull out of the shoot as he asked to speak to Stacy Michaels.

"This is Stacy."

He shifted in his desk chair. Lord, he'd

been alone too long if a woman's voice over the phone could get his imagination and motor running this fast.

"Hello? You still there?"

"Yeah. This Colt Montgomery. I run Healing Horses. I received the paperwork for your brother." He explained about the problem with the class she registered Ryan for. "You'll need to sign him up for our fall class."

"That won't work. I'm in the area to film a movie with Maggie McAlister. In fact, she was the one who recommended your program. I was hoping we could work my brother's therapy session around my shooting schedule. I could just pop over from Twin Creeks, deal with his therapy and then head right back."

Pop over? Did she think Healing Horses worked like the drive-through lane at McDonald's?

"Mr. Montgomery, I'm in a bind here. I can't lose this movie opportunity, but I have to get my brother into therapy. There has to be something we can do."

He'd heard about Maggie filming a movie on Twin Creeks. Since becoming parents, she and Griffin had started a production company and were trying to do more projects at the family ranch when their reality show *The*

Next Rodeo Star was on hiatus. Considering that, Stacy probably was the same woman who'd been one of Griffin's bachelorettes.

He shook his head. His gut told him this woman would be trouble. Stacy was probably a high-maintenance city actress who had people catering to her every whim. That was the last thing he needed, but they weren't talking about her needing therapy. They were talking about her brother.

The application indicated her brother Ryan had been in a car accident a little over a year ago. He'd suffered a traumatic brain injury that left him with impaired gross and fine motor skills as well memory problems. He'd been through two surgeries to correct his crushed legs. Despite that and extensive physical therapy, he still required a walker and struggled with balance and control issues. The kid was only seventeen.

If he told Stacy no, would she make her brother wait to get therapy until she finished her movie? He refused to be responsible for a kid not getting the therapy he needed. "We offer private classes. 'Course that's more expensive."

"Great. Sign Ryan up for that instead."

Not how much more expensive? Must be nice to not have to worry about money. Now him, he pinched pennies until they cried uncle, but he'd do whatever he needed to in order to make Healing Horses work without having the program's needs financially impact Jess's life or her college plans.

"When would you like his therapy to start?" he asked as he jotted down the changes on Ryan's paperwork.

"We'll be in Estes Park Thursday. If he could start therapy next week that would be great. Having private sessions will work better than Ryan being part of a class anyway. I'm going to do everything I can to avoid shooting conflicts, but sometimes my schedule changes at the last minute. I'm hoping you can be a little flexible."

He could see it now, calls with her saying something had come up and she needed to reschedule. Showing up late for appointments because whatever she had been doing ran long. He intended to set her straight up front. "Since we're a new program, our physical therapist and instructors have other jobs. Rescheduling a session isn't easy."

"I'll try my best to avoid any conflicts."

Once he ended the call, Nannette asked, "Was it the same Stacy Michaels?"

"Since she's an actress, I'm pretty sure she's the one you met. I need you to schedule private sessions for her brother. She said they'll be getting into town the end of this week. She'd like his therapy to start next week." He rubbed the back of his neck, where an ache had settled. "Is she as bad as she sounded on the phone? Because she sounded like an arrogant, high-maintenance, huge pain-in-the-butt celebrity."

"When she showed up at the ranch she looked like she was dressed for some fancy New York City cocktail party. She had on this skimpy, skintight dress and these strappy little heels. In Colorado. In December."

His stomach dropped. "What about her attitude?"

"I'm not sure we got to see who she really was. Hardly anything that happened on *Finding Mrs. Right* was real. There were scripts and discussions about what would make good TV. Everything everyone said and did was for the cameras. Her being here will be different. There won't be any cameras. This is real life. Plus, she's not the patient. Her brother is."

"She sounds like someone who creates chaos wherever she goes. We can't let her upset our routine. A big part of our program is having structure and order."

"That's the spirit. You were in the military. Keep her in line."

Of course Nannette, the spokesperson for the United Optimists of America, would think that. He'd been to Afghanistan and faced the possibility of dying on a daily basis, but women? No man could keep one in line.

Stacy had forgotten how beautiful Estes Park was. Even though she wasn't really a back-to-nature kind of gal or the outdoorsy type, the scenery called to her.

The Rocky Mountains stood guard around the small town of Estes Park, almost cradling its inhabitants. That reassuring and enduring presence resonated with Stacy. Something about the wide-open spaces eased the tightness in her chest and stilled her restlessness. The last time she was here she discovered how much slower-paced life was. That had been a huge headache for her. Now it felt as if that was exactly what she needed.

So far settling in had gone smoother than she anticipated. She and Ryan had unpacked and stocked their cabin with food and other staples. They'd met with the school, seen to his registration and he started his first day of classes yesterday. She'd met with Maggie and gotten the shooting schedule so she could schedule Ryan's therapy sessions once they had his initial assessment.

"Now that you've had two days of school, are you sure you want to go Estes Park High? It's not too late for me to get a tutor for you."

"I'm cool with going to school here."

Maybe he wanted a change. Since his accident, Ryan's relationship with his friends was strained. Because he couldn't keep up physically, his friends had moved on. Maybe meeting new people who weren't comparing him to how he used to be would help him come back out of his shell.

"I've actually met a couple of kids. One of them is the daughter of the guy who runs the therapy program. She's in one of my elective classes. Her name is Jess."

So Rooster had a daughter. "What's she like?"

"She's nice. She said she knows what it feels like to be a little different than everyone else."

"What's she mean by that?"

Ryan shrugged. "The kids here aren't as worried about how much money a guy's family has. They're more real."

His phone dinged indicating he had a text. He scanned the message. "It was from Mom. She said she might join us next week. Can you believe it? Does she really think I'll buy that? Next she'll tell me to write a letter to Santa at Christmas." Ryan chucked. "I'd probably get better results from the letter."

"At least she's trying." More like Andrea was saying the right thing. Their mother talked a good game and tossed out big promises. Follow-through proved to be an entirely different matter. "She might surprise us." But only if Grant moved back into the house and agreed to come with her. Otherwise Andrea wouldn't leave California, but Stacy bit her tongue to keep from mentioning that.

"When are you going to quit giving her more chances? She doesn't deserve it."

For Ryan's sake she kept banging her head against the wall in attempt to get Andrea to change. A teenager needed the guidance and love of a parent. He'd changed so much over the past years. Some of it was just normal teenage-attitude stuff, but she knew some of the differences were because of their mother. Every time she disappointed Ryan, every time she put her needs above his, Stacy saw a little part of her brother die inside.

"She's going through a tough time." She regretted her words the minute she uttered them. How could she have been so thoughtless to Ryan when he'd faced far worse than Andrea? "Not like what you're going through, but she's not as strong as you are."

"She's a selfish bitch who doesn't care about anyone but the husband of the month."

Out of the mouths of angry teenagers often came the harsh truth.

Part of her considered talking to him about how families should forgive and love each other no matter what, but she lacked the energy for a battle. Especially when he was right. She'd tried so hard to make up for Andrea's shortcoming so Ryan wouldn't grow up feeling unloved, but there was only so much she could do.

No matter how hard she tried, she wasn't his mother.

Ryan glanced out the window. "Are you sure you know where we're going? I think we went past this barn a little while ago."

Stacy flashed him a bright smile. "I've got everything under control."

No way would she admit she didn't have a clue where they were. She'd never hear the end of it because Ryan had suggested they print a copy of the directions before they left the cabin. Since they were running late, she'd brushed him off saying they'd be fine with her GPS app on her phone. Unfortunately she'd forgotten how spotty Wi-Fi could be in the Rocky Mountains, forcing her to rely on her memory.

"That's your too-big smile. It means you're lying because you're afraid if you tell me the truth, I'll be upset."

"I don't do that."

"You do it all the time. I'm not a kid. I don't need you protecting me."

They'd both grown up too fast. She'd hoped to save him from some of that, but life had a way of refusing to go along with a person's plan.

"Okay, you win. I admit it. We're lost." She spotted a small ranch house in the distance to the left. "I'll head for that house and ask for directions." Then she pointedly stared at her younger brother.

He stared back. His right eyebrow rose and he smiled.

"Are you going to say it?"

His grin widened. "Say what?"

"I'm not going to have an 'I told you' so hanging over my head. Let's just get it over with."

"But it's more fun to torture you this way." His smile faded and he picked at a frayed spot in his jeans. "I know you don't think this horse-therapy stuff is a good idea, but I researched it a lot. I think it could really help me."

Right after the car accident, Ryan's attitude amazed her. He'd been so full of hope. He swore he'd regain full use of his legs no matter what he had to endure. He'd remained positive during his first surgery and the countless hours of physical therapy. Then the doctors recommended another surgery. When he failed to see much improvement after the second operation, something inside Ryan withered.

He quit going out with friends. Though he hadn't said so, she suspected being with them only reinforced what he couldn't do. He argued with her about attending physical therapy.

"I'm tired of doctor and therapy appointments controlling my life. I want to be normal again. I want to hang out with friends, go out on a date or spend the whole day in school without getting pulled for an appointment. This sports riding program is my best bet to have that. I know you're scared because of what happened to dad, but I'll be okay. Everything I read about the program says falls are rare."

But they do occur. She could handle anything but something happening to Ryan again. He was all she had. Her only family. The only one who cared about what happened to her.

No, that wasn't true. Andrea cared about

her, but only because if something happened to Stacy, who would pick up the pieces of her life when it inevitably fell apart?

"I'm praying you're right."

They came around a curve and a loud pop echoed around them. The car pulled hard to the left. Stacy clutched the steering wheel, pulled her foot off the gas and struggled to maintain control. Her sweaty palms slipped on the steering wheel.

"Slow down!" Ryan screamed.

"We're fine." She flashed him a quick smile, hoping to ease his fears and stave off a full-blown panic attack. His fingers dug into the armrest. His breathing grew rapid and shallow. "Breathe slow and deep."

She'd veered into the other lane. She turned hard right. Too hard. The car spun. Ryan's screams reverberated through the car as they headed for the ditch.

Images blurred around Stacy. Her hands grew numb, and then seconds later the car stopped.

"God, no! Not again!" Ryan screamed.

Thank you, Lord. He's yelling. That means he can't be hurt too badly.

Her heart thundering in her chest, her body shaking, Stacy grabbed her brother's arm and squeezed. "Look at me, Ryan. Are you hurt anywhere?" His gaze locked on hers, and he shook his head. "Breathe with me."

She inhaled deeply and held her breath for a second before slowly exhaling. She did that for a minute or two until his breathing matched hers and the panic receded from his eyes. "I'm sorry. I think we blew a tire." She squeezed his hand again before letting go. "You handled that so well."

"No, I didn't. I screamed like a little girl."

"Don't be so hard on yourself. Remember how bad the attack was the first time you got in a car after the accident? You've come so far since then, but that doesn't mean that sometimes you won't get thrown for a loop."

A chorus of moos and clomping hooves on the pavement around them drew Stacy's attention. Not only had they gone off the road into a ditch, but they'd run into a barbed wire fence, taking a good section of it out. Cows making the most of the damaged fence made a break for it and wandered all over the road.

Now what? She put the car into Reverse and tried to back out of the ditch, but the tires spun in the soft ground. They clearly weren't going anywhere.

"I'll go for help."

"What about the cows? We can't leave them all over the road. They'll cause an accident."

She drew the line at worrying about the cows. They'd have to fend for themselves. If they were smart enough to get on the road, they were smart enough to find their way off again. "I bet animals get on the road around here all the time. People are used to watching out for them."

"This is a tourist town. What if someone from out of town comes along? They could get hurt because we..."

Ryan's voice broke. Stacy reached out and laid her hand over her brother's, but he pulled away. This scene was hitting a little too close to home for him. His breathing accelerated again. His pupils dilated.

"Okay. Don't worry." She patted his arm. "Maybe if I lay on the horn they'll move."

The horn's harsh blare hurt her ears, but the cows were apparently hearing impaired because they didn't even twitch. She laid on the horn for a good thirty seconds this time. Nothing.

"Got any suggestions on how to get them to move?"

"Sure. We studied roping cows and ranching in school just last week." Ryan laughed and the tension left his features.

"Smart-ass." Stacy chuckled. This was the brother she loved so much. The one she feared might soon become smothered by his physical limitations.

She glanced at her watch. They were already late for Ryan's appointment. "I could call someone, but we don't have time to wait. We're already running late." How hard could it be to get the cows off the road? "I should be able to take care of this. In one episode of *The Kids Run the Place,* we went for a vacation on a dude ranch. We had a cattle-drive scene."

"That was when you were thirteen. Can you even remember anything from that far back?"

"Gee, I don't know. They say the memory goes the closer you get to thirty. In a couple of years I probably won't even be able to remember who you are." She opened the car door. "Stay here while I get the cows moving. You've been through enough today."

"I'll help."

No way would she risk him getting hurt. They'd pressed their luck enough for one day. "I've got it. There aren't many of them."

"Just because my legs don't work like they used to doesn't mean I can't do something."

So often since the accident she'd felt she lacked the skills to deal with Ryan. At times she had to be mother, cheerleader and therapist. Being a substitute parent to a teenager had been tough enough before his accident.

"I don't know—"

"It doesn't matter what you say. I'm coming."

She thought about pulling rank. With a teenager? They'd only end up having a huge fight and he'd do what he wanted to anyway. "You can help me holler at them, but stay close to the car."

Then she climbed out of the sedan, retrieved his walker from the backseat and handed it to him when he opened the passenger door.

Lost and now chasing cows off the road. Great start to the day. Could things get any worse?

Stacy moved toward the animals. Waiving her arms, she yelled, "Go! Get out of here!"

Joining in the effort, Ryan waved his left arm and shouted along with her.

Of the cows on the road, only one lifted her head and turned in Stacy's direction. Then the animal returned to munching on grass, without moving an inch. She searched her memory for how the cowboy at the dude ranch kept the cows moving. He'd sauntered up to them full of confidence and authority, slapped a lasso against his thigh and hollered at them.

Trying her best to imitate the cowboy's swagger, she moved forward, yelling, "Ya," and slapped her thigh.

"Watch out, Stacy."

She glanced over her shoulder toward her brother and her right foot landed in something mushy. "Ugh!" Her foot slid. Her balance waivered and she felt herself falling. Her backside landed hard against the paved road, but that wasn't the worst part. The unmistakable sour smell of manure wafted around her.

"Are you okay?" Ryan asked.

Really? He had to ask? She was sitting in the middle of cow pie. Of course she wasn't okay. "I'll live."

Though her shoes were goners and probably her jeans, too. She glanced at her favorite pair of shoes, leopard print Louis V stilettos ruined with cow poop, and the dam holding her emotions in check sprang a gigantic leak. Tears stung her eyes. She was so damned tired of being strong, of taking care of everything and everyone around her. Of smiling for the world when all she wanted to say was to hell with it.

The whine of a motor sounded around her. Not a car, but some smaller recreational vehicle. She closed her eyes. A moment later when the noise stopped she opened her eyes to find a hand in front of her face.

"Looks like you could use some help."

Stacy's gaze traveled from the hand—not a well manicured hand like the actors she worked with, but one of a man who worked hard for his living, rough and tanned—to find a tall golden-haired man dressed in faded jeans and a Western plaid shirt standing beside a three-wheeler with a small cart. She grimaced. The only thing worse than falling in a cow pie was having a cowboy with an incredible body sculpted by hard work and piercing blue eyes witness her embarrassment.

"No, I'm good. Just thought I'd sit here and reconnect with nature."

"At least you haven't lost your sense of humor."

Her heart fluttered at the twinkle in his sky-blue gaze. Oh, my. He wasn't even close to her type, but this cowboy definitely had something, and every cell in her body knew it.

Chapter 3

When Stacy placed her hand in his, the calluses on his fingers brushed her wrists. She almost gasped when excitement rippled down her spine. That is, once she recognized the emotion, which was hard to do considering she couldn't remember the last time she'd felt anything resembling interest in a man. Once she could speak, she joked, "Good thing, because my pride's sure shot."

"I bet it'll recover."

Her reaction to the cowboy was out of whack. A born and bred California girl, she'd been attracted to well-built surfer types. Something about their daring, how they challenged those giant waves drew her. Maybe because she'd always been so cautious, but then she'd realized all they cared about was catching the next wave.

She'd dated a few actors she'd worked with over the years. A movie pulled them together, but those relationships never worked. Actors had a way of slipping into their characters almost 24/7 during a film. When filming ended and she came to know who he really was, she often realized she'd been more attracted to the character he'd been playing than the real man.

A few times she dated businessmen, but they became frustrated with the travel and long absences associated with her job, but cowboy guy here? The rugged outdoorsman type never even showed up on her radar. So what about this cowboy got her all hot and bothered?

There was something about his eyes. Clear and blue, they shone with mischief and determination definitely, but something else. The look of an old soul haunted his gaze for brief flashes.

That combination in his steely gaze told her this man would be trouble. No doubt about it.

When the woman at his feet clasped her delicate hand in his, their gazes locked and his breath hitched. Blond hair. Blue eyes that sparkled like a mountain spring under the morning sun. A woman who could look this pretty while sprawled in manure had to be trouble.

He glanced between her and the teenager waiting by the car. A teenage boy who needed a walker. His stomach tightened. Unless Colt missed his guess, Stacy and her brother Ryan had arrived.

He'd expected her to be beautiful because all the bachelorettes on *Finding Mrs. Right* had been knockouts, but he'd expected more California high-maintenance style. Not a woman with natural, understated makeup wearing jeans. Granted they were fancy designer ones with sparkly things instead of sturdy rivets and she had on stiltlike heels, but he wouldn't have pegged her for a Hollywood actress.

After he helped her stand, he reached into his back pocket, pulled out a bandana and handed the cloth to her. "It's not much, but this will let you wipe off a little. I'm Colt Montgomery. Are you by chance Stacy and Ryan?"

"A little worse for the wear, but that's us." She laughed. The rich sound raced up his spine.

Colt strolled to where the teenager stood at

the edge of the road, and shook hands with the kid. This he knew how to deal with. "How about you help me get these knuckle-headed animals back where they belong?"

For a minute the kid's eyes widened with surprise before he masked the emotion, but before he could respond his sister piped in. "I don't think that's a good idea."

The first thing Healing Horses needed to work on was getting Ryan's sister to quit treating the kid as if he would shatter right before her eyes.

"I wouldn't ask if he couldn't handle it."

"You don't know him. I do." She crumpled his red bandana in her fist. "Plus, these cows are huge. What if one of them charges?"

"A car heading straight for them won't budge these things, and you're worried they'd suddenly get the gumption to charge?" He shook his head. City folks and their hare-brained notions. "These aren't the bulls that run in Pamplona."

"I don't know. A couple of them look like they could be troublemakers." One of the cows raised its head and turned toward her. She pointed at the animal. "That one's been giving me the evil eye. I think she has it in for me. Can you personally vouch for her character?"

Her attempt at humor almost made him smile. Almost. This woman appeared to have more than one trick up her sleeve to disarm a man, but then what did he expect from an actress? She could pretend to be anyone she wanted to.

Ignoring Stacy and her pretty blue eyes that he suspected could see straight inside him, he turned to Ryan. "What do you say, sport? You up for this?"

"Just tell me what to do."

"Wait a minute. Are you sure that's a good idea, Ryan?" Stacy stepped forward, but then stopped and smiled at her brother. "Be careful."

"Ryan, you head over there to the opening in the fence. Stand right beside it and make sure the cows don't make a last-minute break for it." Colt knew once he got the animals that far, they weren't likely to find the energy to go anywhere. "They probably won't. It's more likely they'll get all bunched up. If that happens just swat them on the rear to speed them up."

"Got it."

Ryan clutched his walker and tried to find a level spot. Once he did that, he moved his walker and stepped. He repeated the process again. Colt glanced at Stacy. Her gaze locked on her brother as she stood there, her body rigid, her hands clasped in front of her, nibbling on her lower lips. *She wants to help, but she knows he needs to do this on his own. Maybe there's hope for her.*

A couple of steps later Ryan wobbled. Colt glanced again at Stacy. When she stepped forward he shook his head and she froze, concern clouding her beautiful features. Sweat beaded on Ryan's face as he worked his way out of the ditch to the hole in the fence. Once there, Colt walked up to the ring leader and slapped the cow on the hind quarters. "Move!"

In fewer than five minutes he had all the cows back in the pasture. That job done, he tugged the fence until it and Stacy's rental car created a temporary barrier. "This should hold them until Charlie can fix the fence." Colt strolled to his three-wheeler, crawled on and then glanced back at the pair. "Ryan, hop on the back with me. Stacy, ride in wagon and hold the walker."

Ryan headed toward him, but Stacy stood rooted in her spot glaring at him. "Why do I have to ride in the cart?"

"Your butt's covered in manure."

"Ryan, won't you switch—"

"I'm not having manure all over my seat."

She appealed to her brother again.

"Sorry, sis. I'm siding with Colt on this one."

Hands on her hips, she said, "You've got to be kidding?"

"It's either the wagon or walk," Colt replied.

She shook her head, dropped her hands off her hips and walked toward the wagon. "Men."

When Stacy arrived at the Rocking M Ranch she found herself thankful that the jolting ride over in the cart hadn't loosened her teeth.

They stopped in front of a mocha-colored wood-and-brick house with trees that stood guard around the structure. The house, while not huge, wasn't too small, either, and was in pristine condition. When they reached the front porch, she discovered a rocking chair. She could envision Colt's long frame seated there as he surveyed the beautiful land around him.

This wasn't a house. It was a home.

Once inside the living room, Colt turned to Ryan. "You can hang out here while I show your sister where to clean up. Then we'll head for the barn and I'll show you around. We've got a few things to take care of before your first session, like picking out a horse for you."

"Shouldn't I be there for that?"

"He's seventeen. He'll be fine." Colt motioned for her to follow him. "I'd let you use my daughter's room, but you know how teenagers are about their privacy."

At the mention of his daughter, she glanced at his left hand. No wedding ring, but then a lot of guys, especially ones who worked with their hands, didn't wear one. "Ryan said he met your daughter at school. How old is she?"

"Almost sixteen. I've got three months until D-Day."

"Huh? I don't get it."

"She gets to date and drive when she turns sixteen in three months."

"You look tough. I bet you can survive it. I did with Ryan. I'm not saying it'll be easy, but it can be done."

"Guys are different."

She thought about his comment. In some ways she'd had it easier with Ryan. Guys didn't get pregnant. They weren't victims of date rape. There were a hundred other horrors parents of teenage girls had to worry about.

At the end of the upstairs hallway Colt opened the door and stepped aside for her to enter. Stacy walked into the room and stared.

Never in her life had she seen such a neat, well-organized bedroom. Not a speck of dust lay on any of the large rustic furniture. The bed was not only made, but there wasn't a wrinkle anywhere on the dark brown comforter. No clothes on the floor. No shoes for someone to trip over. Not even any change tossed on the nightstand by the massive bed. "Either your wife spends all her waking time cleaning or you've got an amazing maid."

"I'm not married, and you're looking at the maid."

That explained the no ring. Was he divorced? A widower? Whatever his situation, between that and being a war vet, the man probably carried more baggage than a 747. She didn't want to know.

She craved average and uncomplicated.

Knowing about a person's life led to attachments and caring, which led to emotional entanglements, responsibilities and expectations. All of which usually ended up with her getting disappointed. She thought about her past relationships. Whenever she started having expectations or wanted more out of the relationship, her boyfriends suddenly stopped calling.

She and Colt had a business arrangement.

He was to help Ryan overcome his physical disabilities. Period.

But she couldn't miss the similarity of their situations. She was raising a teenage boy and half the time she felt clueless. While he was raising his daughter alone, and from his comments, she suspected he often felt out of his league, too. Men and women saw the world differently, and no matter how she tried, they couldn't really stand in each other's shoes.

She could imagine how much harder it would be for a guy to raise a teenage girl alone. Dealing with female hormones and emotions which caused bigger ups and downs than an amusement-park roller coaster, her developing body *and* the sex talk issues. The man must be made of titanium.

"You need something to wear while your clothes are in the washer." He walked to his closet door. Inside were neatly folded shirts, organized by color, even the plaid ones, stacked on metal closet organizer shelves. He selected one. Then he grabbed a pair of jeans and a belt and handed the items to her.

She stared at him. He was easily six-two and solidly built. "You're kidding, right? Have you looked at me?"

A slow grin spread across his face, as his gaze scanned her from head to toe. And not a quick look, but a slow inspection that let him take his time to check out all the assets. She, who was used to guys staring at her as if they could see through to her underwear all the time in auditions and on the set, blushed at the intensity in this man's gaze.

"What in particular am I supposed to notice?" His low, husky voice slid over her, making her tingle. Really? Tingle? Men didn't make her do that. What was up with her reaction to this guy? He wasn't even close to her type. He was too strong. Too imposing. Just plain too much.

But there was something about him. An honesty and a confidence she found compelling. *He's real. What a woman saw was what she'd get.*

Stop it. He's the last thing you need right now.

She cleared her throat. "I'm built a little bit different than you are."

"Thank the good Lord for that."

She pinned him with her best no-nonsense, we're-not-going-anywhere-on-a-personal-level stare. "These will be huge on me. I'm not sure your belt has a hole tight enough to keep the jeans from falling off. Doesn't your daughter have something I could borrow?"

"I can't loan you anything of Jess's without written permission. My luck, whatever I gave you would turn out to be her favorite pants. You'd fall in another cow pie or snag them on something in the barn, and I'd be a dead man."

His words said with a straight face and a tinge of fear rippling in his voice made her smile. Humor? What an odd, but not unpleasant, combination with his take-charge attitude.

"You're afraid of a sixteen-year-old girl?" she teased back.

"Damn right. You were that age once. Don't you remember what you were like with your clothes then?"

"What was I thinking?" At that age she'd been on a hit TV series. Her image had been everything, and yes, she'd been fanatical about her clothes.

"A smart man knows when not to press his luck." He took the clothes from her and placed them on his enormous bed. Then he pointed to the door opposite the closet. "There's the bathroom. The towels are in the linen closet and the soap's in the shower. My robe's on the back of the bathroom door. Try the clothes or put on the robe. I don't care which."

Then he told her where to find the washer and dryer, and said to join him and Ryan when she could. He was out the door before she could even comment.

Stacy found Colt's bathroom in the same pristinely clean and organized fashion as his bedroom. After she washed up, she grabbed the forest-green terrycloth bathrobe off the hook and slipped the garment on. An earthy smell mixed with a spicy scent flowed over her as if the man had wrapped her in his strong arms.

Not good.

Wearing his robe was way too intimate. She smoothed her hand down the fluffy fabric. How could she feel a connection with a man by putting on his bathrobe? It was silly, but in slipping into the garment, she felt exactly that—connected.

A vision of Colt, strong and confident, standing in this room, wearing this same garment filled her vision. While the robe reached her ankles, the garment would hit him just below the knees. She could see him, the robe gaping to reveal his muscled chest, standing in front of the sink shaving that stern chin of his. Then she saw his clear blue eyes focused on her as a woman in this room.

Wrong move. Afraid of the ache pulsing in her body, she scooped up her dirty clothes and headed for the bedroom door. She had to get out of his room. Intent on escape, she flung open the door and almost barreled into a dark-haired teenager with caramel-colored eyes, a Chihuahua clutched in her arms. Except for her strong chin, she looked nothing like her father.

She must be the exact image of her mother.

"Are you Jess?" After the teen nodded, Stacy continued to introduce herself. "I'm Ryan's sister. Thanks for showing him the ropes at school."

"He told me about the movie you're making. I can't wait to see it in the theater. Maggie said I can be an extra in a couple of scenes."

Not knowing what else to say, Stacy said, "Cute dog. What's its name?"

"Thor."

"That's an interesting choice for a name."

"I know. It drives people crazy." Jess tossed Stacy a saucy grin. "You were one of the finalists when Griffin was on *Finding Mrs. Right*."

"That was me."

"Getting dumped on national TV had to suck."

Sure did. Thanks for bringing up the pleasant subject. Being on that show and some comment about the disastrous finale would end up on her tombstone. Some bad decisions kept on giving. "It wasn't a lot of fun. For a while I was the punch line to some pretty nasty jokes."

"It hurts when you get made fun of for someone else's choices."

She knows because she's been there. The words to ask what had happened with Jess sat perched on her tongue. No, she wouldn't ask. No attachments, remember? She was only here for ten weeks. Get in. Do the job. Get Ryan the help he needs and get out.

"Luckily there's a new scandal every five minutes in Hollywood, so everyone moved on pretty quickly."

"Dad sent me to see if you need anything."

"I'm good, but thanks for asking." Stacy nodded toward the wadded clothes in her hands. "I was just going to put these in the washer. I'm not sure I can salvage them, but I'm going to try."

"I heard about your fall. The first thing I learned when we moved here was to always watch where I step."

"I could've used that info earlier," Stacy joked as she followed the teenager downstairs to the utility room where they tossed her clothes into the washer. "I'm a little taller than you are, but I could also use something to wear. Maybe some sweatpants and a T-shirt? Your dad said he couldn't loan me anything of yours without written permission."

"He knows better than to mess with my clothes. One time I put a load of my stuff in the washer before I left for school. He came along and put them in the dryer. I didn't talk to him for a week after my favorite jeans shrank so much I looked like I was ready for a flood."

"That hurts. A shirt can be replaced. That's easy, but jeans?"

"I know. It's about impossible to find a pair that fit right and look good."

Stacy nodded in feminine understanding. "Guys don't get that."

"Especially a cowboy. Any pair of Wranglers is fine with them." Together they headed upstairs again. When Jess opened the door, Stacy realized looks weren't the only way this girl differed from her father. Clothes, books and papers littered every surface. Obviously she hadn't inherited her father's neat-freak tendencies.

After digging through her dresser, Jess pulled out a pair of gray knit yoga-style pants and a plain white T-shirt. "These should work and don't worry about getting them back to me right away. I only wear them to sleep in."

"Thanks. I want to see how Ryan's doing,

and I can't go to the barn in a bathrobe."
Jess handed her the clothing. "Your dad said
I could put on a pair of his jeans and one of
his shirts."

Jess laughed. "Sure, that would work. The
pants would end up around your ankles."

"That's what I said." Stacy shook her
head. "His solution was to hand me one of
his belts."

"My dad's a great guy, but sometimes he's
such a *guy*."

That was one thing Colt Montgomery was.
All man.

In the barn, Ryan leaned on his walker and
looked at Colt. The haunted look in the teen's
gaze reached out to Colt, reminding him of
the look he used to see in Reed's eyes at that
age. This kid had seen way too much and
been hurt a time or two.

"Thanks for telling my sister to lighten up.
She's gotten a little overprotective since my
accident."

"I picked up on her being the worrier type,
but I bet it's only while she's awake."

Ryan smiled, and some of the tension left
his face. His shoulders relaxed, too. "She's always watched out for me. Our dad died when

I was a baby and our mom's worthless. It was just the two of us."

Like him and Reed. Two kids clinging to each other through the storms of life that tossed them around. Now her protectiveness made sense.

"That's why we went to court to get her named my guardian."

Colt wondered about why she'd legally taken on the parent role with her brother when he read the application. That told him a lot. How many sisters would do that? She could've turned eighteen, moved out of the house and went on with her life without giving her brother much thought. She could've left him to fend for himself.

Like he'd done with Reed.

Until recently, Colt hadn't known how bad things had been for his brother after he left home and enlisted. One night things got so bad Reed nearly beat their old man to death. Then damned if the bastard didn't want to press charges for assault. If it hadn't been for Nannette's husband, Ben, Reed would've been arrested for assault. Ben McAlister had been one damn fine man. He'd been there for Reed when Colt hadn't been.

Unlike him, Stacy stuck around for her brother.

"She's especially concerned about me doing this therapy," Ryan continued. "Our father was thrown from a horse on a movie set. That was how he died."

"And she's letting you get on a horse? How did you talk her into that?"

"It wasn't easy, but she knows this is my best chance to walk on my own again."

Still, that took guts on her part. Then he thought about the movie Maggie was making, *The Women of Spring Creek Ranch*. "The movie she's starring in is about female ranchers. Won't she have to ride a horse for the movie?"

"She said none of her scenes have anything to do with horses." Ryan's hands tightened on the walker handles. "Do you think you can help me get rid of this thing?"

"A local physical therapist and I went over your doctor's report to develop activities geared toward your physical issues. I can't promise you'll get rid of that thing by the end of your sessions, but I know we can help you."

"I bet you're wondering why I'm here, cause you see people who are so worse off than me."

"Everyone has the right to get the most he can out of his life. We help whoever needs us whether it's a little or a lot." He motioned for Ryan to follow him. The tap-scrape of the walker echoed through the barn. "Being a teenager is tough enough without having to deal with medical issues. What were you into before the accident?"

"I ran track and played basketball. My friends and I used to rock climb a lot."

The unsaid words hung in the air between them. *And now they do, and I can't.*

"I have a couple of good buddies who were hurt in Afghanistan. It's a tough adjustment. It changed their lives completely."

Being there changed mine, too. Just not in the same way.

"I'll give you the fifty-cent tour," he said to Ryan. "We'll get some of the busy work out of the way. Then you can have your first session tomorrow."

Colt led Ryan into the tack room in the center of the barn where the shelves were stacked with helmets. He handed one to the teenager. "Try this on."

"I'm seventeen and have to use a walker. Now you want me to wear this? Dork of the month calendar, here I come."

The kid still had spirit. Good. That would work in his favor. "Sorry. It's the rules. Every rider wears one."

Ryan tossed on the helmet and snapped the

chin strap. "If a picture of me in this thing ends up on Facebook, I'll kick your ass."

Colt laughed. "Fair enough." Then he checked the fit. Two tries later, and they had the right one. "Our next step is picking out a horse for you. How tall are you? About five-eleven?"

"I guess."

"I think you and Chance will get along well. Come on. I'll introduce you." They walked through the barn to the horse's stall. The animal sauntered over and pressed his nose against the window bars. Colt rubbed the animal's head. "You ever been on a horse before?"

Ryan shook his head and moved closer to the stall. "Can I touch him?"

Colt nodded, and explained what the therapy would entail. "You two are going to become good friends. You'll be working on using your body to direct Chance. That will help you regain control of your own body."

"Ryan, where are you?" Stacy called out.

"Over here," Ryan responded.

"We're in the first row of horse stalls."

A minute later she joined them, but she shied away from the stall door, keeping as close to the larger open area as possible. "I see Jess loaned you some clothes." Ones a bit too small for her. His daughter's knit pants and T-shirt molded to Stacy's lush figure, leaving no doubt about her feminine curves. A body like hers could make a man break out in a cold sweat and damned if Colt wasn't doing just that.

"This is Chance," Ryan said as he stroked the gelding's head. "Colt thinks he and I will do well together."

Stacy leaned forward and glanced in the stall. "He seems nice, but isn't he awfully big? What about another horse? A smaller one?"

She had the nerve to question his judgment about horses? That hit a sore spot. "We may be a new program, but we *have* done this before. Ryan's not our first client."

"I didn't mean to offend you or criticize the program. This is all new to us, and I have some questions. Maybe you could set aside some time to talk with me about my concerns."

"Send me an email and I'll answer them the best I can." Stacy might have let her brother sign up for the therapy, but her watching him mount a horse wasn't going to be easy. Colt's job was to make sure she didn't interfere with his program or Ryan's therapy. Somehow he didn't think that would be simple, either.

"I'd rather talk in person, especially since I'm here right now."

Colt glanced at his watch. "Ryan and I are done here, and I've got to get ready for my group class, so let's see how tomorrow goes. If you still have questions after Ryan's first session then we'll talk."

As Colt walked away he couldn't help but think that Ryan's sister was a worrier, and no doubt about it, the woman was trouble.

When Stacy and Ryan returned to Healing Horses the next afternoon for his first therapy session, the coffee she downed at lunch to perk up churned in her stomach, leaving her queasy. For the past twenty-four hours she kept telling herself Ryan would be okay. That nothing would go wrong, but doing so failed to keep her nightmares in check. They started out with her as a child with her father. Then a giant horse materialized. Its enormous hooves crushed her father before her eyes. Fog floated in as she raced to him. By the time she reached his body, she found herself kneeling over Ryan.

She wished Colt had been willing to talk to her about her concerns before Ryan started therapy, but he'd fobbed her off instead. That made her even more edgy.

As they made their way toward the barn, Ryan glanced at her, his eyes filled with concern. Now she'd done it.

"Are you going to be okay? I know how hard this is for you, but I'm not going to be doing any crazy stunts on the horse. The most I'll be doing is walking around trying to get Chance to go from one side of the ring to the other. If things get really wild I might stop somewhere and throw some bean bags at a target."

He shouldn't have to worry about you. Pretend you're in a movie. Slip into the role of a big sister who's sure everything will be fine and doesn't have a care in the world.

'Course it might take a performance worthy of an Academy Award, but she'd give it a try. "Sounds pretty tame, almost boring." She smiled and tried to relax her shoulders. She was hunching them again. "It's not so much that I'm worried about you. I'm just tired because we ran so long shooting yesterday."

At least that part was true.

"Colt's going to be mad that we're late."

"I couldn't help it. The director switched the shooting schedule on me."

By the time they reached the barn, she'd managed to get her nerves under control, at least outwardly.

Colt met them inside the door, his arms crossed over his broad chest, a frown darkening his handsome features. "You're late."

Ryan glared at her. "I told you he'd be mad."

"It won't happen again." If she could help it.

Colt led them to a small room with a battered leather couch, an equally beat-up fridge and a TV. "Here's the family waiting room. Ryan will be back in about an hour."

"You expect me to stay here? I want to be there during his therapy."

"That's not a good idea."

"I don't need you there to hold my hand, Stacy."

No, Ryan didn't. This wasn't about what he needed. Despite knowing that, she couldn't stem her concerns now that she was here.

She ignored her brother's comment and addressed Colt instead. "I didn't read anything in the material you gave me that said I can't be present during the session."

"Most people take my word for it when I've said it's better if they wait here."

Everyone else hadn't watched their father get trampled to death. "I'm not most people. Now we can stand here wasting more of everyone's time or we can get on with Ryan's therapy. Which is it going to be?"

"We'll give it a try, but there better not be any trouble."

When they reached the mounting block area in the barn, Colt introduced them to Nikki, the young woman who would be the leader for the session, and her friend Sarah, who'd act as the sidewalker. Then Ryan clip-clopped up the steps to stand on the block. When Nikki led the massive horse, saddled and ready to go in front of him, Stacy started chewing on her lip. She knew from her research what everyone's job was, but that failed to ease her anxieties.

From the information she'd read on Healing Horses, she knew Colt was a registered instructor. That meant he ran the session and worked with a physical therapist to create a program suited to Ryan's needs. He was trained. Certified. Regulated. But the others helping with the session were volunteers.

The leader's responsibility was the horse. This volunteer maintained the horse's pace and kept the animal calm. The sidewalker's role was to help the client with balance. But Stacy couldn't let go of the fact that they were volunteers. How much experience did this skinny cowgirl have? She was only a couple of inches taller than Stacy's own five foot six, and couldn't be more than twenty-one. "Colt, excuse me. Can I talk to you for a minute?"

Was that squeaky, panicked voice hers?

He stalked over. "First of all, calm down. If your voice gets any higher only dogs will hear it." He nodded toward the horse. "If you get upset and agitated Chance will sense that."

"Then maybe he's not the right horse for Ryan. I know I mentioned this yesterday and you weren't concerned, but he seems even bigger out here than he did in his stall yesterday. Don't you think Ryan might need a smaller horse?"

The bigger the horse, the more damage he could do if something went wrong.

Colt shifted his stance and stiffened. "Chance is the right size. Ryan's a big kid."

"What about your leader? Is she capable of controlling an animal that size? How much experience does she have?"

"Nikki is a champion barrel racer. She's been around horses all her life. There isn't one in the state that she can't handle."

"Why is there only one sidewalker?" Often clients had two people to focus on them, help interpret instructions and provide physical and emotional support.

Instead of answering her, Colt walked to

Nikki and whispered something. Then the woman led Chance away. When he stalked to Stacy, determination filled his gaze. He closed the distance between them in two long angry strides.

"We need to talk." Colt clasped her upper arm and tried to lead her away. When she attempted to pull away, he stopped, leaned down and whispered in her ear. "We can do this one of two ways. You can come with me of your own free will, or I can toss you over my shoulder. Which is it gonna be?"

"You wouldn't."

"Try me."

Chapter 4

Colt knew he needed to nip the situation with Stacy in the bud right quick. This first session would set the tone for every one to come. With Stacy more jittery than a mama bear with her first cub, they'd never get around to helping Ryan.

Stacy stared at him for a minute with hard determination and he thought she might defy him. That might not be a bad thing. The thought of getting his hands on those great curves of hers did have a certain appeal and could end up being the bright spot in his day.

"Lead the way," she conceded at last, leaving him a bit disappointed.

Once they rounded the corner out of sight

and earshot of Ryan and Sarah, Colt said "I want to make some things clear. Once the horse is in front of the mounting ramp, the therapy session's started. Other people talking confuses the animal. The leader and Ryan should be the only one giving commands."

"What if—"

"No, what-ifs. Those are the rules. It's for everyone's safety. When you're around the horse, you need to remain calm, quiet and not make any sudden movements. It can make a horse shy or kick out."

"I admit I'm a little nervous."

"You'd have to take a Xanax to get down to nervous."

"I wasn't that bad."

He crossed his arms over his chest, leaned back on one heel and tossed her a she-had-to-be-kidding look.

"Okay, maybe I was getting a little overly—" She paused, obviously trying to find the right word.

"Panic stricken? Paranoid?"

"I'll dial it down. I'll really try."

The pain in her voice took the wind right out of his sails. This had to be so hard for her. He'd forgotten what she'd gone through with her father. Only a complete ass would be this harsh on a woman in this situation.

"I know this is tough for you. Ryan told me what happened to your father. How a horse trampled him to death on a movie set. What you're feeling is understandable."

She paled and her shoulders hunched, leaving her looking vulnerable and small. Almost alone against the world. "Everything I read about programs like yours says falls are rare, but they do happen. I can't get that out of my head."

"Ryan's got more physical control than most of our clients. He's got better chances of getting hit by lightning than falling off a horse. What happened to your father won't happen here."

"My head knows that, but my heart can't let go of my fear. He's all I've got."

That he could understand. While she wasn't Ryan's parent, she and Ryan had that kind of relationship. What if he'd seen a loved one get trampled to death and then someone wanted to put Jess on a horse? "It's hard, but you can't let the past and your fears affect Ryan's therapy. Go to the waiting room. Turn on the TV and forget about what's going on. It'll be better for everyone. You included."

She stiffened. Her back ramrod straight, her gaze tossed daggers at him. He'd sure hit a nerve. It was almost as if what he said made her mad. As if he'd called her weak, and now she was out to prove she could handle this, but danged if she wasn't even prettier with her dander up.

"He's my brother. I'm his guardian. It's my job to watch out for his best interests and to ask questions."

So much for the understanding, soft approach. "You're getting in the way."

"You can't make me leave."

"We know what we're doing."

"Then you shouldn't have a problem with me asking a couple of questions because you can explain your actions with sound reasoning."

The woman had grit. He had to give her that. Normally he admired that trait, but right now her tenacity had given him one monster-size headache. "I'm willing to talk about your concerns, either before or after the session."

"But what if something comes up during the therapy?"

"I'll deal with anything that comes up. That's my job. If you can't follow my rules, find another program for Ryan." They both knew there wasn't another therapy option that would allow her to continue working on the movie. "Now what's it gonna be?"

Defeat crossed her delicate features. "I'll be

quiet. I promise, and I'll keep my questions until after the session is over."

Damn. He felt like the playground bully who'd chased the prettiest girl in class, knocked her down and left her with a skinned knee. "I'll give you one more shot."

After they returned to the mounting area where Ryan and Sarah waited, he motioned for Nikki to return with Chance. Before Colt could get them moving toward the ring, Stacy's voice stopped him. "Are you sure Ryan doesn't need two sidewalkers for safety purposes?"

"So much for being quiet." He glanced at his watch. "That lasted less than two minutes."

"His therapy hasn't started."

"One sidewalker is plenty." He motioned Nikki to keep coming.

Chance sensing Stacy's anxiety tossed his head and she jumped back. "I don't think this is the right horse for Ryan. The animal seems awfully nervous."

Knowing he needed to get control of the session and eliminate the problem, he stormed toward Stacy. "I warned you."

"What are you doing?" Eyes wide, she stepped back.

He took a minute to calm down before answering. Then in a measured voice he said, "You being here isn't good for anyone. Not the horse. Not Ryan, and certainly not you."

That pretty little chin of hers pointed at him in defiance. "I'm not leaving."

When he'd closed the distance between them, he lifted her into his arms and slung her over his shoulder. Damn she was tiny, barely weighing more than his favorite saddle. She pounded on his back, but he barely noticed. A mosquito had a bigger bite. "Chance is a calm horse. It's you who's making him act like he is. Hell, you're making everyone nervous."

"Put me down. You can't do this."

"Seems I can." He continued walking. When she squirmed in his arms, he tightened his grip around her shapely legs and then swatted her on her tight little butt. "Settle down. I don't want to drop you."

"That's exactly why you should put me down. That and the fact that you don't have any right to do this." She went limp in his arms, though anger still rang out in her voice, loud and clear. "Why is it you keep telling me what to do? You are the most arrogant, presumptuous man I've ever met."

"My ranch. My rules." He stomped out of the barn and through the arena toward a small grassy area with a picnic table. He deposited her on the other side of the short fence. "Stay here and keep quiet. If you don't, the next step is locking you in the tack room. Understand?"

She wobbled and grabbed the fence post for support. Then she looked up at him with what he could only describe as terror in her eyes. "Tell me Ryan will be okay and that nothing bad will happen."

Her voice, soft and scared, reached inside him and squeezed. He placed his hand over hers. When heat shot through him with more force than a bull bent on ridding himself of a rodeo rider, he pulled back. "We know what we're doing. This is a different situation than a movie set. I won't let anything happen to Ryan."

The trust in her eyes almost bowled him over. He refused to let her vulnerability get to him. She was an actress. Who knew how much of what he saw was real and how much was a show staged to get her way? "Stay here and be quiet. If you can't handle that go to your car or the waiting room."

"But what if—"

"You take care of the problem or I will, and you won't like my solution. I guarantee it." For the next hour, Stacy rode a roller coaster of emotions as she stood on the grassy area outside the arena and watched Ryan work to control his body and direct the horse around. A few times he'd wobble in the saddle making her hold her breath and clutch the bench underneath her, but he quickly stabilized.

At those times, Colt never even flinched. Just looking at him, all arrogant and confident, sent irritation coursing through her system. She wasn't sure what to make of him. First of all, he'd gone all caveman on her and thrown her over his shoulder, making her angrier than she could ever remember being.

But she wasn't sure who she was madder at—him or her.

Admit it. You liked having a strong man's arms wrapped around you.

She scoffed at the idea. Being a take-charge guy was one thing, but Colt took that to the extreme. How dare the man tell her what was best for her brother? He hadn't been with Ryan through all the surgeries and physical therapy. Colt hadn't seen how the lack of progress destroyed his spirit. She knew her brother better than anyone and what was best for him.

But as Ryan's therapy session progressed, she found herself admitting Colt appeared to know what he was doing. He offered suggestions on ways Ryan could improve his control and balance. He complimented her brother on what he did well.

After the session ended and they stood back in the barn after Ryan dismounted, Stacy found herself more than a little shaken, and not just because of her concern for her brother. She wasn't sure how to process the emotions Colt aroused in her.

Forget about Colt and concentrate on the fact that Ryan had survived his first therapy session without incident. Now she had to lay the groundwork for the future ones.

"Ryan, help Nikki and Sarah groom Chance and put away his gear."

Her brother glanced between her and Colt. "You aren't going to kill each other, are you?"

"All I want to do is talk to her," Colt replied in an even voice.

Ryan turned to her as if waiting for her confirmation. "Go. Colt's right. We need to discuss some things."

Once the others left she spun around to face Colt, her anger returning. "Don't you ever manhandle me again like you did today."

"I owe you an apology."

Talk about a shot out of the blue. She hadn't expected that at all. She figured he wasn't a guy used to having his authority, his rules or his decisions questioned. After all, he was ex-military. Weren't they all about structure, order and following the status quo?

When did men, even non-military ones, ever admit their mistakes? *And you've had so much experience with men,* a little voice inside her taunted. At least the actors and male directors she worked with over the years never admitted their mistakes, but men outside of the entertainment industry? She admitted the data was a little sparse.

"I'm usually a pretty even-tempered guy, but I was so all-fired mad I couldn't see straight." He ran his long fingers through his sun-kissed blond hair. "And obviously I wasn't thinking clearly."

That made two of them. "I have to ask questions. I'm responsible for Ryan. I have to watch out for him."

"You're worried about him falling. I get that, but you don't understand. What you were doing increased the risk of that very thing happening."

His words hit her like a hard punch to the stomach. Had she really done that? The thought left her weak. She clasped her hands in front of her to keep them from shaking.

"So where do we go from here? I have to be with him."

"It would be better for you both if you weren't there."

"Let me rephrase that. I *will* be here while he's going through his sessions."

"I'll make a deal with you. I'll train you like any other volunteer. If you pass the muster and agree to follow the rules like everyone else, I'll let you be Ryan's sidewalker. That should give you a greater sense of control."

No. She couldn't do that. Horses were huge, unpredictable, and the thought of being that close to one left her shaking in her Louis V's. "I can't do that. I wouldn't be any good. Just the thought of being near a horse makes me physically ill."

"A person's fear over something is usually worse than facing it. Being in a war zone taught me that. You can do this."

The faith and certainty shining in his cycs bolstered her courage. When had anyone believed in her other than to think she could pull off a role convincingly?

She would do this for Ryan. Then she could be there with him. She could support him and understand what he was going through. "I'll do it."

"So we're clear, you'll have to follow the same rules as any other volunteer. That means

I'm the boss and you do what I say, no questions asked."

She nodded. "When can we start?"

"When do you have a day off from shooting?"

"Saturday."

"I'll see you here at eight. Don't be late." He pointed to her fancy high heels. "And get some decent boots."

A few days after his run-in with Stacy, Colt picked Jess up from school and she asked if she could go to Halligan's that night. "A bunch of the kids are meeting there to listen to Maroon Peak Pass. I really want to go. Not only because my friends are going, but I want to support Emma."

Jess met the band's lead singer and guitarist while volunteering at the Estes Park animal shelter, where Emma worked as the volunteer coordinator. "Is Cody one of the kids that'll be there?"

She shrugged. "I didn't ask, and I don't care."

His throat tightened. "Did something happen on your date?"

"He seemed like such a great guy, but he was a bore."

That he could handle. "I wish I could say

that would be the last boring date you'll go on, but it won't be."

"You mean I have to kiss a lot of frogs before I find a prince, kind of thing?"

"You kissed him?"

"No." She drew out the word so it sounded more like *no-ah*. Translation: Dad, you're being such a jerk. "All he did was talk about himself and how great he was. Why would I kiss him after a date like that?"

She was growing up so fast in some ways and still so young in others. "You think you could make time to have dinner there with your old man before you meet your friends?" The remainder of Stacy's first week in Estes Park passed by uneventfully after Ryan's therapy. Amazingly, Ryan loved Estes Park High School. He'd come home talking about the kids he'd met and was actually excited. He said it was almost freeing not having anyone know what he'd been like before the accident. His life was a blank slate now and he could make it whatever he wanted.

"Everyone says there's a great band playing at Halligan's tonight," he said the minute he climbed into the car after school.

"What kind of band? Country, I'm guessing."

He nodded.

"Since when are you interested in country-and-western music?"

"I don't care about the music. I just want to hang out."

"I can drop you off. What time do you want to go?"

"I was hoping you'd go with me. You could use some fun, you know."

"Okay. What's up? No teenager wants to go to hear a band with his sister. Even one as cool and wonderful as I am."

"Don't go, then. Sit home alone. What do I care?"

Then the reason for his request hit her. How could she have been so stupid? Ryan wanted to fit in. He'd already bought a closet full of Wranglers and ditched his fancy sneakers for cowboy boots. She bet he was uneasy about going alone. He wanted her there as a safety net. "You're right. I do need to get out. How about we go for dinner and then stay to hear the band?"

An hour or so later after she'd cleaned up and changed, she and Ryan walked into Halligan's Bar and Grill to find the restaurant packed.

The last time she'd been in town, she'd kept to herself. Since her lodgings possessed a kitchen she'd hidden out there, living on whatever she could throw together or ordering from whatever places delivered, but this time was different. She couldn't crawl into her cave. Not when Ryan wanted to belong so much.

Heads turned as they walked in. Stacy smoothed a hand over her blouse.

"I told you you'd be overdressed." Ryan warned her that Halligan's wasn't like the restaurants and clubs she went to in L.A. She'd stubbornly told him she was who she was and she wasn't about to change. Now she wished she'd reconsidered.

Halligan's was a Wranglers, cowboy boots and cotton shirt type of place, and whether you were a man or woman that was the dress code. Dressed in a burgundy silk blouse, designer jeans and stilettos, she stuck out like a dandelion in a clover field.

The place had a down home kind of charm with its Formica-topped tables, neon beer signs and wood floors. Families sat at some of the tables. Friends at others. Some people shot pool or tossed darts in one of the game rooms. The stage and dance floor took up one end of the restaurant. The tantalizing smell of fried food wafted through the air, making her stomach growl. How long had it been since she'd had anything fried?

Definitely not since she starred in *The Kids Run the Place*. The producers had been sticklers about her weight. Once her mother found that out she'd instituted daily weigh-ins and kept a log of every bit of food that went into Stacy's mouth.

When she asked for a table for two, the perky little cowgirl hostess informed them it would be about an hour before she could get them a table. Stacy turned to her brother. "How about we go home, grab something to eat and come back to hear the band?"

"I guess so," Ryan answered, disappointment filling his voice.

As they turned to leave, someone called his name. "Hey, there's Jess and her dad." Without even asking if she minded, he maneuvered his walker around the tables toward them, leaving Stacy no choice but to follow.

She hadn't seen Colt since Ryan's therapy, and wasn't prepared for how at ease and how handsome he looked. Tomorrow when she met him for her volunteer training she'd be ready, but not now.

"We just ordered, but you can join us. Can't they, Dad?" Jess said.

Colt nodded as he shifted in his chair. "Sure." His tight tone told Stacy he wasn't any happier about this than she was.

"Great," Ryan said, and plopped his long body into the chair beside Jess.

"We don't want to intrude," Stacy said in a last-ditch attempt to get out of the situation, but her brother and Jess were already in a deep discussion about the merits of tonight's band.

"It's a lost cause. They aren't listening." Colt slid the remaining chair away from the table. "If I promise to be good and not to throw you over my shoulder again, will you have a seat?"

I don't want you to be good. I want to feel your arms around me again.

Where had that thought come from?

Stacy no sooner sat down when Jess and Ryan stood. "We're going to play darts. Text me when my food comes. I'll come get it. Ryan can order his food in the game room." Then the teenagers left before she or Colt could protest.

Once alone silence settled around her and Colt. She toyed with the plastic menu. Talk about awkward. The last time she had a first date hadn't been this uncomfortable. That's the problem. With the teenagers gone this felt like a date. Not good. She needed to get out of here quick.

Since Ryan had found Jess to hang around

with, Stacy could go home and curl up on the couch to watch a movie. That's what she should do, but somehow the idea sounded much better earlier. Now her plans sounded— pathetic.

"I'm going to leave. I can pick up Ryan later."

Coward.

Yup.

Colt's hand covered hers when she tried to push away from the table. The simple contact sent shivers through her. They both jerked away as if they'd touched a hot stove. When was the last time she felt this kind of excitement with a man?

Way too long.

His blue gaze locked on her. "You can't leave me here to eat alone. First Jess dumps me and now you want to. A man's ego can only take so much." He had the most soul searching eyes. They could strip a girl defenseless in seconds. "Stay."

Her mouth went dry. Her heart rate skyrocketed.

"All right. I'll make the sacrifice so you don't have to sit here alone." She picked up the menu, thankful that her hands didn't shake.

"Who's your friend, Colt?"

The waitress, a curvy blonde in jeans so tight it was a wonder she could walk, strutted up to their table. She eyed Colt as if she was a five-year-old birthday girl and he was one of her presents.

"Jenna, this is Stacy Michaels. Her brother, Ryan, and Jess are friends from school."

"I thought you looked familiar. You were one of the finalists in that dating show Griffin McAlister was on."

Here we go diving headfirst into the most embarrassing experience of my life.

"I was."

"Were you the one who caused the horse to bolt and left Griffin in the hospital or were you the one who threatened to sue him at the finale?"

While what she'd done was embarrassing, at least Stacy's actions hadn't landed Griffin in the hospital and temporarily paralyzed. She should have expected to encounter some resentment toward her because of what she'd done to one of the town's favorite sons, but the animosity still caught her off guard. She plastered an I-refuse-to-let-your-insult-get-under-my-skin smile on her face.

"It really doesn't matter," Colt interjected. "That's in the past. Everyone's moved on. In fact, she's got the lead role in the new movie Maggie's filming."

Stacy stared. He defended her?

"That's so like you, Colt. You're always one of the first ones to say forgive and forget." Jenna smiled at Colt. Could this chick lay it on any thicker? And he didn't even seem to notice the woman drooling over him.

The waitress's grin disappeared when her gaze focused on Stacy. "What makes a woman go on a dating show? I mean, to compete with other women for a guy that you've just met and let the whole world watch? That doesn't seem the best way to find a man."

No kidding, and any woman who thought it was needed serious psychotherapy. There was a reason why those relationships rarely lasted. They weren't based on things that mattered like shared values and respect. Those bedrocks kept a couple together through life's ups and downs. But what could she say to little miss cowgirl?

Avoid the issue. That's what she'd do.

"You know, Jenna, as wonderful as it is chatting with you, with the crowd in here tonight you've got to be incredibly busy. I don't want to monopolize your time, so I'll give you my order so you can be on your way. I'll have a veggie wrap."

"A veggie wrap?" Colt scoffed. "You need some meat on your bones. You look like a strong wind would blow you over. Halligan's is known for their burgers." Colt turned to the waitress. "Get her a buffalo burger instead."

What was it with this guy telling her what she should or shouldn't do? She'd been taking care of herself since she was eleven. "I ordered a veggie wrap because that's what I want. I don't eat red meat."

"Any fries or onion rings to go with that?" Jenna asked.

Stacy bet Halligan's had killer fries. Probably crunchy on the outside and all warm on the inside and the thought of onion rings left her weak. "No, thanks."

"Don't tell me. You don't eat fried food, either," Colt said.

"As a matter of fact, I don't." While the business had loosened up about actresses' weight— Melissa McCarthy winning an Outstanding Lead Actress in a Comedy Series Emmy was groundbreaking—the rule still was the more a woman weighed, the fewer scripts crossed her agent's desk.

Jenna jotted down Stacy's order on her little pad and then glanced longingly at Colt. "Are you staying to dance tonight? I get off at nine."

"I haven't planned that far in advance. I know it doesn't look like it right now, but I'm here spending time with Jess. She and Stacy's brother are playing darts."

"How's she doing? A girl needs that strong female presence in her life, especially when she's a teenager." Jenna's eyes widened as if she'd realized how what she'd said could be taken as a criticism of Colt's parenting skills. "Not that you aren't doing a great job as a parent. It's just sometimes a girl needs to talk to another woman."

"Luckily Jess has Avery for that."

Stacy perked up at his comment. Who was Avery? His girlfriend? An unfamiliar emotion she refused to label jealousy snaked through her.

It's none of your business who he's dating.

Someone from another table called the waitress. After Jenna promised to check back with Colt later and reminded him to "holler" if he needed anything, she sashayed off.

Once they were alone again, Stacy said, "Thanks for saying something when she started in on the dating show stuff. It gets old having to explain that I'm over what happened. I don't know why everyone thinks I'm carrying a torch for Griffin."

"Since you brought it up, why did you go on that show?"

Stacy leaned toward him. "I'll be honest with you, but you can't ever tell anyone."

"You can trust me to keep your secrets."

The joking tone in his deep voice contrasted with the sincerity shining in his eyes. The breath caught in her throat. What would it be like to have someone to share her deepest dreams and fears with? Someone who after he heard all that, still cared for her.

Big wrong turn.

Time to fix her mistake before she went much further down this road and ended up in another ditch. Ignoring the feelings he brought to life inside her, she said, "I was between jobs, and needed to jump-start my career. I don't care what they tell the media, no one goes on a dating show expecting to fall in love and have the relationship last. It's all about creating a career or advancing one."

She traced circles in the condensation on her water glass. "My plan was to get some valuable TV exposure so I could get a network interested in giving me my own reality show. The good news was I did that. The bad news was my show was a miserable failure."

"I don't get the fascination with reality shows. Why would people want to watch other people living their lives rather than going out and living their own?"

"I guess some of the allure is because people can be part of lives they could never have. You know the rich and famous or the wild and crazy stuff. That and we've become a voyeuristic society."

"Did you always want to be an actress?"

His question hit her right between the eyes, startling her, mainly because she'd never thought about it before. Had she ever really had the opportunity to choose her career? "Jeez, this is starting to feel like you're interviewing me for an article."

"I'm just curious. I really want to know."

Genuine interest? In her as a real person? It had been so long since she'd experienced that.

Stacy explained how she'd fallen into her career when her father recommended her for a role in his last movie. "Spending that time with my dad was so wonderful. Then he died." She bit her lip to control the ache unfurling inside her heart. "After that, I got the chance to do the series *The Kids Run the Place,* and I had a career."

"I remember that show. It was great. You starred in that?"

She nodded. After the series took off she never had the chance to step back and decide if acting was what she wanted to do with her life. "My mom was in charge of my career then. I didn't have much choice. I was the family breadwinner."

"That's a lot for a kid to handle."

By then she wasn't a kid anymore. She smiled at the strong man across from her. "Your turn to be in the hot seat. What made you start the therapy program?"

How long had it been since she'd sat with someone and talked in something more than sound bites? Really shared something personal and real about herself? When was the last time someone, especially a man, made her want to talk about herself, and she'd felt genuine interest in his life? More importantly, how long had it been since a man had showed a real interest in her as a person?

Not good.

Don't look in his eyes and you'll be okay. It's his eyes that get a girl.

A man was the last thing she needed in her life right now. Not with her mother on the constant verge of a nervous breakdown, her career needing another serious boost to refill the family coffers, and a brother in physical therapy. She couldn't care about anyone else now. That would send her right over the edge.

Too bad she felt so wonderful talking with

Colt, being honest. Sharing. Because she couldn't afford the luxury of feeling anything for him.

Chapter 5

Colt hadn't been thrilled when Jess invited Stacy and Ryan to join them for dinner, not after how the first therapy session went. The woman had him alternating between wanting to throttle her and scoop her up in his arms. And not just to haul her off. When he'd told her how her behavior could get Ryan hurt, she'd looked so vulnerable and frightened. Anyone who loved another person as much as she loved her brother had to possess a good heart. He'd wanted to hold her and ease her fear. He longed to tell her everything would be okay because he'd make sure of it.

That thought scared the hell out of him.

But now that they'd started talking, he

found himself having a good time and she appeared genuinely interested in what made him start Healing Horses. "A buddy of mine got hurt pretty bad in Afghanistan. His doctor recommended a horse-therapy program, but there wasn't one close to where he lived. I figured I had the barn, the land and horses. Why not do some good with them?"

"Was it bad in Afghanistan?"

His tour was the last thing he wanted to talk about. He tried hard to put that part of his life behind him. "You know how you get tired of everyone asking about when you were on *Finding Mrs. Right?*" She nodded. "That's how Afghanistan is for me."

Jenna arrived with their food before Stacy could respond. The waitress again asked if he'd thought any more about his plans. He mumbled something about he still wasn't sure and she said she'd check with him after her shift ended.

"Are you going to take our waitress up on her offer?" Stacy asked.

"What offer?"

"Come on. You can't be that clueless. She so wants to jump your bones."

"Jenna? No. You're wrong. I've known her forever. There's nothing between us. I've never thought of her in that way." The thought of dating a woman who'd trailed after him and her brother didn't feel right. Kind of like kissing your sister. If he'd had one.

"You may not have, but I can guarantee she has."

"The one woman, or rather young lady in my life is sometimes more than I can handle right now. Add to that getting Healing Horses off the ground, and I've got enough responsibilities to keep me on the edge of insanity. Which reminds me, I need to text Jess that her food's here."

Grateful for the task, he pulled out his phone and sent the message. A minute later, his daughter arrived, scooped up her plate and left again.

"I understand. It's hard being responsible for a child of the opposite sex. I try my best to understand things from Ryan's perspective, but no matter how hard I try I can't stand in his shoes."

"That's for sure." Clothes, menstrual cycles, dating. Enough to drive a father screaming into the night. "I think you've got the easier deal. Guys are simple. Women are complicated."

"You've got to be kidding? Guys are easy? You don't want to talk about anything, especially your feelings. You just get mad. With

Ryan sometimes I think the only way I could figure him out was if I was a mind reader."

"That sure would come in handy."

They continued talking about the kids while they finished eating, and when the band started warming up, Jess and Ryan made their way back to the table. "We're going to sit with some friends and listen to the band. Are you two sticking around or will you be coming back to pick us up?"

"I thought we'd come and sit by you two," Colt said with a straight face. When horror crossed his daughter's face, he chuckled. Sometimes it was just too easy to pull her chain.

"Dad, you wouldn't?"

"'Course not. Though the thought of torturing you like that does sound fun." He turned to Stacy. "Want to stick around and listen to the band for a while?"

"Might as well. All I'd do otherwise is go back to the cabin and watch TV until I had to pick Ryan up."

Once seated at a table around the dance floor, Colt noticed Travis Carpenter kept eyeing Stacy like a stallion watched the mares in the next pasture. Carpenter's behavior shouldn't have bothered him, but it did. Probably if it were anyone else he wouldn't care.

You are so full of it, and you know it.

Carpenter had been a blowhard from the day he strutted into Colt's kindergarten class. Though he'd been shorter than most of their classmates, even then he'd possessed enough ego for the entire class. Seemed from then on they competed over everything. Who could run faster, who could get the better score on a test, who could get the prettiest girl in the class to go out with him. Colt won that contest in high school when Lynn dumped Travis to go out with him, putting them on the outs for good.

Now Colt sat here at a table with Stacy, not knowing what to say or do with Travis watching the whole embarrassing display. What did he expect when hadn't been on a date in over sixteen years?

When the hell had he started thinking of this as a date? Damn. He should've left when they finished eating and come back to pick up Jess. He still could. A smart man worked to fix his mistakes before they bit him on the ass.

"Eight o'clock is gonna come awfully early—"

"Hey, little lady," Carpenter said as he materialized beside their table and introduced himself. "Since Montgomery here isn't asking you to dance, how about you and I take a turn around the floor?"

Stacy lifted her feet and pointed to her strappy little high heels and pouted. "Unfortunatcly, I didn't wear my dancing shoes tonight. Maybe next time."

"It's a slow one. All you need to do is hang on to me."

Travis swayed slightly. Colt glanced at the man's eyes to confirm his suspicions. Yup, he'd had too much to drink. "The lady said not tonight."

"Stay out of this, Montgomery. This is between me and the lady here, and I didn't hear the word *no*." Travis stepped closer. "I didn't realize it until I got up close. You're the actress that was on that show with Griffin."

Stacy nodded and smiled, but it wasn't an open, heartfelt one like he'd received earlier. This smile failed to make her eyes sparkle. "That's me, and apparently my only claim to fame."

"McAlister was an idiot to let you go, especially for that plain mouse he married. If you've still got a hankering for a cowboy I'm up for the job."

Colt shook his head. What woman wouldn't be thrilled with that offer? Protective feelings surged within him again. What was it about this woman that brought that out in him? "Go home and sleep it off, Carpenter."

"I don't hear her complaining."

"Gentlemen, dial back the testosterone," Stacy teased, in an obvious attempt to ease the brewing tension. "It's getting a little deep in here."

Carpenter clasped Stacy's hand and tried to coax her to stand. "Come on. How about that dance?"

Stacy glanced between him and Carpenter, concern furrowing her brow. "One dance, but that's it."

"You don't have to dance with him."

Stacy smiled and waved him off. Once on the dance floor, Carpenter's meaty hand slid around her waist and he pulled her against him. Too close. Stacy playfully swatted his arm and tried to put some distance between them. Colt scooted forward in his chair, waiting to see the other man's response. Then the man's hand slid to Stacy's rear, cupping and then squeezing her feminine curves.

Colt vaulted out of his chair and headed for the couple. As he approached, Stacy grabbed Carpenter's hand and attempted to remove it. "Get your hands off my butt."

"Come on, honey. You're a Hollywood

actress. Don't play modest," Carpenter responded.

"That's it. We're done." When she turned to leave, Carpenter refused to release her. If anything, he tightened his grip.

"You promised me a dance."

Colt closed the distance between them in two long strides. "Let her go."

Travis glared at him over Stacy's shoulder. "You gonna make me?"

"This isn't about you and me. The lady asked you to let her go."

Stacy tried again to break free, but Carpenter only smiled. "You promised me a dance, and it's not over yet."

"Yes, it is." Stacy stomped down on Carpenter's foot with her pointy little heel and elbowed him in the ribs.

After Stacy broke free, Carpenter lunged toward her, but Colt stepped in front of her. The other man lowered his shoulder and barreled into him, sending him careening into a table. Couples scrambled to get out of the way. Women shrieked.

White-hot rage darkening Carpenter's features, he reached for Colt again, but Stacy grabbed his arm. "Stop it!"

"Dad, are you okay?" Colt cringed when he heard his daughter's voice as he struggled to free himself from the overturned furniture. Before he could, Carpenter hauled him to his feet. Having reached the limit of his patience with talking to the drunk, Colt managed to turn around and get Carpenter into a control hold.

The drunk kicked and thrashed around, trying to get loose. "Montgomery, I'm going to take you apart."

Carpenter's boot connected with another table, sending it tumbling over. Glassware shattering against the wooden floor added to the chaos. "Settle down, and I'll let you go."

A shrill whistle cut through the chaos, followed by Mick Halligan's harsh voice. "This damned well better stop right now. You two go to neutral corners and park it. I've called the police, and you can bet your sweet ass I'm pressing charges." Then Mick glanced at the band. "Show's over. Let's have some music."

As Colt sat at the table waiting for the police to arrive, he couldn't believe he'd gotten into a bar fight with his daughter around to witness his stupidity. Great example he'd set for Jess, he thought as he rubbed his aching jaw, but when Carpenter put his hands on Stacy he couldn't think about anything but helping her.

And look where it got him? Waiting to see if he'd get thrown in jail.

"Jess, I don't want you thinking using physical force to solve problems is the right thing to do."

"Dad, you don't need to make this a teachable moment. Mr. Carpenter was crazy out of control. His hands were all over Stacy. I mean, he was grabbing her ass."

"You saw that, huh?" Stacy asked, blushing.

"I did, too." Ryan turned to Colt. "If you hadn't done something, I was going to. Someone had to show that bastard he couldn't treat my sister like that."

At least he'd kept Ryan from having to defend his sister. Even drunk, Travis would've pounded Ryan into the floor.

"I think you did the right thing helping Stacy. It wasn't your fault he threw the first punch. After that you were just defending yourself," Jess continued.

But would the police see it that way? Where had his military training gone? He should've assessed the situation and the risk before he acted, but when Travis started pawing Stacy, all he wanted to do was protect her.

A few minutes later the front door swung open and in stalked what looked like half of the Estes Park police force. Chief Parson immediately talked with Mick. After a short discussion, the chief told his officers to get statements from the patrons. Then Parsons headed straight for their table.

"Can we talk about this somewhere other than in front of my daughter?" Colt asked when the lawman reached them.

Of course, since Jess witnessed the whole scene, he was trying to close the window after the house was full of flies.

"I agree. These youngsters don't need to hear this." The chief moved a few feet away with Colt and Stacy. Then Parsons said, "I hear this ruckus started because two men were arguing over you."

Stacy stiffened, crossed her arms over her chest as her eyes flashed fire at the lawman. "That's right. I turned on my feminine wiles and stirred both men into such a frenzy they ended up brawling over me."

"This isn't Los Angeles. You might be some fancy star there, but that doesn't mean a thing to me, so don't get smart with me, Missy."

"Then show me some respect, and don't assume I did something wrong."

Colt bit his lip to keep from smiling. It sure

was easier to appreciate her stubborn feistiness from this side of the conversation.

"Fair enough," Parsons acknowledged. "Tell me what happened."

"We were sitting at a table—"

"I want to hear this from her, Colt," Parsons snapped.

Stacy detailed how when she and Ryan arrived tonight the wait for a table was almost an hour and how Jess had invited them to join their table. "The kids wanted to stay for the band, but didn't want to actually be seen with us. You know how teenagers are." The lawman nodded. "Colt and I sat at a table where we could keep an eye on Jess and Ryan. When Travis came over it was obvious he'd had too much to drink. He asked me to dance, and I politely declined. He wouldn't take no for an answer and got confrontational. I decided the best way to get rid of him was to humor him, but once we got on the dance floor his hands were all over me. When I tried to leave he wouldn't let me go."

"That's when you stepped in?" Parsons asked Colt.

"He was manhandling her. I told him to let her go."

"None of this was Colt's fault," Stacy continued. "If Travis had let me leave the dance floor when I wanted to, the fight wouldn't have happened. He threw the first punch."

The chief shook his head. "Travis doesn't surprise me. He's always been a little long on temper and short on common sense, but you, Colt? This isn't like you at all."

No kidding.

"I don't have any choice but to haul you and Carpenter in to get your statements and sort this out." The lawman rubbed the back of his neck. "Mick's pretty pissed about the damage. He wants both your heads, and Carpenter's hollering for you to be arrested for assault. I should let both of you cool your asses in a cell for the night. That would fix your wagons."

"Travis deserves to go to jail. He started all this, but not Colt. He's done nothing wrong. All he did was help me." Stacy's voice rose in pitch as her anger boiled over. "If he hadn't stepped in who knows what I would've had to do to get Travis to back off. You didn't see the look in his eyes. I guess the lesson here is the next time a man takes liberties with a woman, the men around here shouldn't offer help because it could land them in jail."

"Jack, cut me a break. I'm here with Jess, for God's sake." Colt's voice and gaze pleaded with the chief.

"Even more reason to toss you in jail. You

should set a better example for your daughter." Chief Parsons shook his head. "If I don't haul you in every hothead in town will think he can use his fists to settle a problem."

"If you arrest Colt, I'll contact my lawyer immediately and the press. I'm sure TMZ would love to do a story on this."

"Is that a threat?" Parsons asked.

"It's a statement of fact."

Colt placed his hand on her arm, pulling her attention from the lawman. A shudder rippled through him. "It won't come to me getting arrested. I'll go to the station and get this sorted out. What I need from you is to take Jess home. Stay with her until I get there." He had to get Stacy out of here before she made a scene. This was his home and he had to live here once she returned to California. "Please?"

She nodded, thankfully picking up on his unspoken plea. "But if charges are filed, I want to know."

On the way back to Colt's house with Ryan and Jess, Stacy tried to minimize the situation. She explained how Colt agreed to go to the police station to give a formal statement. She chose her words carefully and emphasize that he hadn't been arrested.

By the time they arrived at the house exhaustion set in. Even the kids looked weary. When they mumbled something about waiting up for Colt, Stacy said, "Taking statements and sorting things out could take a while. It's silly for us to wait up. You can get all the details in the morning, Jess." When the teenager looked as if she wanted to protest, Stacy added, "Ryan can crash here on the couch and I'm going to sleep in the chair. I'm exhausted."

"If you're sure I don't need to worry about Dad."

They'd finally hit the problem. How could she have failed to realize how concerned Jess was? The girl hid her emotions well. "I promise there's nothing to lose sleep over."

She'd call in favors and threaten to blast the story from coast to coast if she had to in order to keep Colt out of jail.

Some of the panic left Jess's gaze. "Ryan can use the guest room."

"Great." He turned to Stacy. "Then you can take the couch."

After the teenagers headed upstairs, Stacy turned on the TV and curled up on the couch. What a night. She still couldn't believe Colt defended her. Not once, but twice. For once in her life someone stepped up and handled something for her.

His actions still left her a little tingly inside. True gentlemen, especially in her business, were as rare as an exotic dancer with real breasts.

The little voice inside her said she was being foolish. She'd watched enough Westerns to know about the cowboy code and protecting womanhood at all costs. Plus, Colt was a military man. Didn't they all have that black-and-white sense of right and wrong ingrained in them during basic training? That's what brought about his actions tonight. He wasn't standing up for her because he cared for her. He would've done the same thing for any woman.

But what if he'd stood up for *her?*

No, she refused to think about that possibility. If she considered dating anyone, he'd be someone who'd never been married before. He definitely wouldn't have children, much less a teenager. He'd probably be a man who was in the entertainment industry. One who could understand the demands of her career. One who would be comfortable accompanying her to movie premiers or the Academy Awards. She couldn't see Colt putting up with the red carpet pomp and circumstance.

But she kept coming back to how he'd stood up for her. She'd felt protected and safe. Something she hadn't felt since her father died. And what did he get for his efforts? He got hauled off to jail.

A couple of hours later, cowboy boots clicking across the wood floor woke her. She opened her eyes to find Colt towering over her.

"Thanks for staying with Jess."

"I'm not sure if I told you, but thank you for that what you did tonight. If I didn't seem grateful, it was because I was a shocked."

"I didn't mean to scare you. I'm not usually the kind of guy who gets into a bar fight."

"It wasn't that. I was surprised because you stepped in. I've learned to be pretty self-sufficient over the years.

"That doesn't say much about the people in your life." He sank into the chair to her right and pinched the bridge of his nose.

That was for sure. "I'm sorry helping me got you into trouble."

"Do you stir up this much trouble everywhere you go, or am I just lucky?"

He turned toward her, and she noticed his swollen and cut lip. "You're hurt."

He shrugged. "When Travis landed that sucker punch, his damn college ring cut me."

"You should put some ice on it to keep the swelling down."

She jumped off the couch, took a couple of steps and realized she had no idea where the kitchen was located. "Where's the kitchen?"

"I don't need any ice. I'm fine."

That he was. Absolutely fine with a capital *F*.

"At least let me clean the blood off and put some antiseptic on your cut." She reached into her purse sitting on the floor, pulled out her little first aid kit and located a foil packet with an antiseptic wipe. When she stood beside him, she leaned over and dabbed the white square to the cut that started on his lip and extended about an inch onto his chin. His spicy scent floated over her, igniting her senses. The stillness in the house created an intimacy she hadn't felt in a long time. "I feel like I should be doing more to make this right. If I had handled things better with Travis... I should've been able to get rid of him. What can I do to make this right?"

His crystal blue gaze darkened. "You could kiss my sore lip and make it all better."

At first she thought he was joking, but then she looked into his eyes. No mistaking the desire shining there. Blood pounded in her ears. She shouldn't kiss him. She knew that, but she wanted to. Desperately. She wanted his arms around her. She wanted to pretend he'd protected her because he cared. That he cared about *her*.

Common sense told her to jump off the couch and run as fast and as far from Colt as possible.

Instead, she leaned forward and touched her lips to his jaw. Then she kissed him lightly on his lips.

Chapter 6

Colt tossed out the "kiss and make it all better" comment expecting Stacy to toss a joke right back at him or put him in his place. His heart nearly stopped when she didn't do either of those things. Instead her lips covered his, and his body shifted into overdrive.

Her hands clutched his shirt and he wrapped his arms around her tiny frame. Her sweet floral scent floated over him. He felt alive. The need to be closer to her overwhelmed him. He missed having a connection with a woman. Sure he had friends and his brother, but there was something about having a woman in his life. They saw things, they understood on a different level, offered a comfort a man couldn't find anywhere else. A soft place to fall.

"Better?"

"My lip's better, but certain other parts ache like crazy."

He lifted her onto his lap. His hands framed her face as he kissed her. He could lose himself in her so easily. She slipped her hand under his shirt, warm and searching. His breath hitched. Her seeking fingers brushed over one of his scars. "What happened here?"

"I got hurt."

"No kidding. It's a scar. Did you get it in Afghanistan?"

He didn't want to remember how Sanders had been blown apart and pieces of his buddy's bones had slashed through his chest. To distract both of them, he nibbled on the sensitive skin below her ear. Her groan rippled through him.

"Never mind." She leaned forward and kissed his puckered flesh. His hands buried in her hair, the silky texture teasing his fingers as heat blasted through him. Unable to bear more of her tender exploration for fear of embarrassing himself, he pulled her face to his.

His lips covered hers again, hungry and almost desperate. Her hands fisted in his shirt as she clung to him. Through a haze, he heard a door creak upstairs, followed by the click of dog nails and the slap of bare feet on the wooden floor. The sexual fog surrounding him evaporated. He lifted Stacy off him and dumped her on the couch. Her hair mussed from his hands, her skin flushed from his touch, her hands shook as she adjusted her blouse. Much longer and her shirt would've been on the floor.

How could he have forgotten his daughter and her younger brother slept upstairs? The woman, her intoxicating kisses and her magic hands could make a man forget to breathe.

A minute later Jess stumbled into the living room, her dog Thor trotting behind her. She glanced between him and Stacy.

He was busted. How the hell was he going to get out of this mess?

Stacy wanted to run for the front door the minute she saw Jess, but running would only make her look guiltier. Nothing to do but straighten out her big girl panties, or in this case her twisted blouse, and bluff her way through the situation. That was it. She was an actress. She'd pretend nothing happened. Play it cool, and Jess wouldn't realize a thing.

Right. Even Meryl Streep couldn't pull off that performance.

Jess glanced between her father and Stacy. A knowing grin spread across the teenager's face. "I guess I interrupted something."

"No, I just got home," Colt muttered as he shifted his stance like a kid caught in a lie.

"I was asleep on the couch. I woke up when the front door closed. I'm a light sleeper. Then I wanted to talk to your dad about what happened at the police station, so we were sitting here talking."

So much for playing it cool. Shut up, Stacy. You're rambling and making the situation worse.

"I'd have to be blind to believe that bunch of BS."

Stacy cringed and refused to meet Jess's gaze.

Great acting job.

"What was or wasn't going on here is none of your business." When Jess opened her mouth to say something else, Colt shook his head. "Don't push me. My patience is wearing thin."

"I can't believe this, Dad. After the lecture on dating you gave me the other day? I guess this is one of those 'Do as I say, not as I do' moments." Then she walked over to her father, kissed him on the cheek and darted out of the room, her dog trotting behind her.

"I didn't think there was anything more embarrassing than my parents catching me making out with my first girlfriend. I was wrong."

"I can't believe—" Stacy paused, wanting desperately to fan her heated face. *I can't believe we acted like a couple of horny teenagers.* "You're right about that."

He shoved his hands in his jean's pocket and shuffled his feet. She stood, not knowing quite what to do now. Finally she said, "I'll wake Ryan so we can go home."

"Let him sleep. Not point in closing this door now that the horse has gotten out of the barn. You can either sleep here on the couch, or I can bring Ryan home when he wakes up."

This time she listened to her common sense. "Dropping him off tomorrow would be great."

As Stacy parked by the Healing Horses barn, she told herself she could do this. She could face her fear of horses. Then she almost laughed. Today facing Colt seemed scarier than facing a horse.

She'd kissed him last night. Not he kissed

her. Well, not at first anyway. No, she'd been the aggressor.

How would she face him? Pretend last night never happened.

Like you pretended nothing happened when Jess caught you two making out? Because that worked so well.

When she walked into the barn, instead of finding Colt, she discovered Jess. *Please don't let her bring up the other night.* "Where's your dad? He agreed to train me to be a side-walker so I can help with Ryan's therapy. I don't want him thinking I'm late."

"Yeah, that's one of his pet peeves." Jess crossed her arms over her chest, and Stacy braced herself and resisted the urge to squirm. This was not good. "What are your intentions with my dad?"

She'd known whatever Jess had been going to say would be something she didn't want to hear, but never in her wildest nightmares had Stacy's thoughts gone to "What are your intentions?"

Beam me up, Scottie. Where was a good Chief Engineer with a transporter when a girl needed one?

Stacy's tongue stuck to the roof of her dry mouth and her mind raced to come up with a plausible answer. Intentions? As in for the future? Damned if she knew. While she might not know that, she'd sure known what her objective had been last night. She wanted to get hot and heavy with Colt.

She couldn't exactly tell his daughter that.

Honesty. They say it's the best policy. She could tell Jess the truth about the future at least. "I'm not sure what's going on between your father and me. We're so different, but when you and Ryan were in the game room last night we talked. I enjoyed his company. He's a nice guy, but we barely know each other."

"That's not what it looked like in the living room."

"It's not—"

"I'm not stupid. You two were getting pretty cozy."

Anyone over the age of five could've figured that out. "I won't lie to you. We were kissing, but that was it."

Only because you showed up.

"He hasn't dated anyone since my mom died almost three years ago."

"Her death had to be hard on you both."

"You have no idea. You can't tell him I told you, but I think you need to know. My mom didn't like it when Dad was in the military. She said she was sick of moving all the time. So he left the Air Force, joined the National Guard Reserves and we moved back here where he grew up."

"But he went to Afghanistan recently, didn't he?"

Jess said he'd been in the National Guard Reserves until a year ago. "Him joining the Reserves was their compromise, but Mom wasn't happy with that, either, or with living here. Then one day she left me a note. She said she was in love with someone else. She said she was sorry to leave me, but she had to take this chance to be happy. She hurt Dad so bad. He tried not to let me see, but I could tell. He was different. I don't know how to explain it."

Colt's wife had an affair and ran off with her lover?

Stacy's heart cracked for both the teenager and the man. The woman had left not only her husband—from what she'd seen at Halligan's, a wonderful, caring man—but her child, as well? A daughter who needed her, who loved her, who counted on her mother to be there for her. Didn't she have any idea of the pain and trauma that caused?

Jess stood there, her arms crossed over her chest, her brown eyes hard as she fought to hold back her tears.

I thought my mother was bad, but she at least stuck around. The woman was a fool and didn't deserve Jess and Colt. She'd been given two precious gifts, and she'd thrown them away with the wrapping paper.

"It wasn't your fault she left."

"I know that." Tears sparkled in Jess's eyes. She bit her lower lip. "The last thing I ever said to her was what a terrible mother she was and that I hated her. Then she died in a car accident."

Jess would never have the chance to take back those angry words. She'd never be able to repair her relationship with her mother, or even find closure. Such a huge burden for such a young woman.

The crack in Stacy's heart widened as Jess's pain reached out to her. She wrapped her arms around the teen, but Jess stiffened and pulled away. "I know you feel guilty about what you said to your mother, but I'm sure she knew it was the anger talking—anger you had every right to feel, by the way—but you've got to let it go."

"But how?" Tears now rolled down Jess's pale cheek.

Damn Jess's mother. How could she do this to her child? How could she choose a lover over this wonderful young woman? "I wish I could tell you. All I can say is that my mother and I haven't always gotten along, but she knows I love her. I'm sure your mom knew that, too. Focus on the good memories you have of her, of the special times you had together." *Please, Lord, let there be some good ones this dear girl can hold on to.* "Your mom wouldn't want you to be feeling guilty. You've got to forgive yourself for what you said. Don't let what happened between you rule the rest of your life."

Like my mother's ruling mine.

No. Don't think about that. Focus on Jess.

Jess swiped her sleeve over her eyes. "Because of what happened with my mom, I'm a little protective of my dad. That's why I asked about what's going on between the two of you. I don't want him getting hurt again."

Which was exactly what Stacy would do if she and Colt got involved. There was no avoiding it since she was only here for a few weeks. On top of that, she couldn't handle a romantic relationship. Hers invariably ended badly, and she was barely staying sane dealing with her current responsibilities. Even if they agreed up front to keep things casual and fun, she wouldn't risk them getting attached—either her to them or them to her.

She refused to leave him and Jess like his wife had.

"You're a pretty great young lady. Your dad's lucky to have you."

"Yes, he is, and if you hurt him, you'll answer to me. Got it?"

"Message received. I have no intention of hurting your dad. We come from such different worlds. All I can ever see between us is friendship."

Chapter 7

Colt walked into the barn and heard the tail end of his daughter's conversation with Stacy. *The last thing I ever said to her was what a terrible mother she was and that I hated her. Then she died in a car accident.*

His daughter's words sliced through him. He'd never known about Jess's last conversation with her mother. She'd been carrying so much guilt, and he'd been clueless. He almost charged forward, but then Stacy's words stopped him. *It wasn't your fault she left.* He could tell Jess all day long not to feel guilty, but she needed to hear that from someone else.

As he listened to Stacy talk to Jess he realized for someone who lived in Hollywood where honesty and being real could be deadly to a career, Stacy did a damn fine job dealing with Jess. Unless this was an Oscar-worthy performance, Stacy truly cared about his daughter.

He and his daughter had both kept secrets. The day before Lynn died she'd called him, too. Things weren't going so well with her lover now that they were playing house. She thought she'd made a mistake. Could she come home?

His first reaction had been to tell her hell, no, he wouldn't take her back, but then he thought about Jess, and he changed his mind. Instead he told Lynn he'd think about what she said and call her in a couple of days, but he never got the chance.

He'd often wondered if he'd told her she could come home would she still be alive. Even if their relationship hadn't worked out, Jess would have her mother. His fear of getting hurt again, of looking like a fool robbed his daughter of that opportunity.

And now she was protecting him.

All I can ever see between us is friendship.

His male pride stung knowing that Stacy could so easily dump him into friends-only status, but that was for the best. Considering what Lynn leaving had done to Jess, he wasn't sure he ever wanted to bring another woman into her life. Maybe once she went off to college he could find someone to share some time with, but not now. He wouldn't risk Jess getting attached and getting hurt if his relationship fell apart.

If Jess wasn't attached to Stacy before today, she probably was now.

He shut the barn door hard enough to alert Jess and Stacy to his presence. "You ready to get started on your training?"

"Absolutely." Stacy posed and pointed to her boots. "See, I remembered to get boots."

Gazing at her standing there in jeans, a simple white blouse and cowboy boots—not fancy ones with lots of color and handwork like he'd expect her to wear, but simple sturdy ones—got his motor running. She looked so blasted cute and proud of herself. Standing there before him she looked so right here, her bright smile lighting up the barn.

Keeping his mind on business was so much easier when she wore fancy rhinestone jeans, an expensive silk blouse and those skinny little heels. Then it was easy to remember she belonged in California. Now, not so much.

He smiled at the memory of the strappy heels she'd worn. Those weren't so bad. They had a way of making her hips sway in a way that mesmerized a man. He swallowed hard.

"It's good to know you can follow directions."

Her bright smile faded, and damned if he didn't feel as if he'd stolen a kid's Halloween candy.

"I think she looks great," Jess said. Then her cell phone rang. When his daughter stepped away to answer the call, he and Stacy stared at each other for a minute, before he said, "You ready to get started?"

"No, but let's get going anyway."

"Ryan's on the phone," Jess said when she returned. "He and I talked about the volunteer work I do at Aunt Avery's shelter, and he wants to go with me for my shift today. Is that okay with you, Stacy?"

"It's fine with me if your dad doesn't mind waiting to start my training until I get Ryan and drop him off."

"You don't need to take him to the shelter. My aunt's picking me up, and we'll just swing by and get him."

After Jess went outside to wait for her aunt, Colt said, "We'll work with Babe. She's a sweet little Haflinger cross pony we use with young riders."

"I'm not sure I can do this. I couldn't sleep last night because of the nightmares."

"I think it was Mark Twain who said, 'Courage isn't the absence of fear, but the mastery of it.' We'll start slow." He led her down the row of stalls. "Weird noises, or loud, excited voices can make the horses nervous. Keep your movements slow and deliberate."

They stopped at a stall about halfway down a long hall. "Hey, Babe. Come here and show Stacy what a sweet girl you are."

The pony trotted over to the bars. He rubbed the golden animal's head. "There isn't a horse that doesn't like having its head caressed. Come here and give it a try."

Stacy shook her head, her eyes wide, her chest rising and falling with her rapid breathing. He stepped away from the horse and moved closer to Stacy. "Relax. Breathe with me."

His gaze locked with hers as he breathed deeply and evenly, until she started calming down. "She's still in the stall. The bars on the door and windows are sturdy, and I'm here. Nothing is going to happen."

"You promise?"

The words hung between them. He couldn't do anything but nod. Hell, he could barely breathe.

She turned away from him and inched forward toward the stall. He scooted closer, needing to offer support. Her delicate fragrance teased his senses. She always smelled like the bouquet of spring flowers his mom used to put in a recycled can vase he made her in first grade art class. He leaned closer and whispered in her ear. "Talk to her."

"Hi." She reached out, her hand shaking. The horse whinnied, and she jumped back, bumping into him. His arms wrapped around her waist to steady her. Physical awareness slammed into him, strong and potent.

He released her as if he'd grabbed a barbed wire fence. *Get yourself under control. You're not a horny teenager.*

No, just horny.

Abstinence was going to kill him.

Lord, don't think about that.

What was he doing? Oh, yeah, getting her comfortable with the pony. "Babe was just saying hello. See how her ears are forward, but relaxed?"

"If you say so."

"That just means she's interested in what's in front of her. You're someone new and she's curious. There's nothing to be afraid of."

At least for her. Him, he wasn't so sure of. His body was running hotter than a thoroughbred after a mile run. "Talk to her like you would a friend."

She inched forward, a look on her face as though she was heading to the dentist for a root canal, but damn, the woman had guts. For him that was far more intoxicating than her beauty. Looks faded. Character lasted.

"Hi, Babe. I'm Stacy. Go easy on me. I'm a little nervous." This time when she reached out, she rubbed Babe's forehead. The animal leaned into her, and she relaxed.

"See, she won't bite your arm off."

"That's good to know."

"If you're good to a horse, he'll be your friend for life. They're pretty easy to please."

Just like me.

He reached into his back pocket and pulled out a carrot. "Give her this."

Stacy stared over her shoulder at him. "I don't know. You sure she won't bite?"

Babe wouldn't, but he wasn't so sure about him. The urge to nibble on that spot on her graceful neck where her pulse throbbed as fast as hummingbird wings nearly over-whelmed him.

Instead, he placed the vegetable in her hand and then covered her hand with his. He stood beside her as they held the treat out to Babe, who snatched up the carrot.

"If you're anxious about working with a horse, it never hurts to bring a treat."

"I'll stop at the grocery store on my way home."

He let go of her hand, and stepped away. Friends. Remember? That's what she wanted to be. That's where he needed her to stay—safely in the friendship zone. He cleared his throat and returned to why she'd come today—her training. "Because of your issues, we won't have you do anything to get the horse ready for the lessons. I'll take care of that. I want you to feel comfortable around the animals, but your job during therapy will be to help Ryan with his balance and reinforce instructions. You'll walk beside Ryan. If you sense he's struggling with his balance, you place a hand on his ankle or his belt until he's steadier."

Before he could say anything further, her phone rang. She grabbed her cell out of her back pocket. "I should check and make sure it's not Ryan."

Colt nodded. "We'll take a short break."

Maybe then he could cool off. He almost laughed. Cool off? Only if he took a second cold shower.

Stacy's heart sank when she glanced at her phone after Colt walked away. Her mother.

She considered letting the call go to voice mail, but Andrea would keep calling until she answered. Better to deal with whatever molehill her mother had turned into Mount Everest as quickly as possible. "Mom, this isn't a good time. Can I call you back later tonight?"

"This can't wait." Her mother's high-pitched, frantic voice jumped across the phone line. Stacy closed her eyes and sighed. Nothing ever could with Andrea.

"There's water all over the garage. I don't know what's wrong or what to do."

"Can't Grant help you take care of it?"

"He's at a friend's running lines to prepare for the audition he has on Monday. I can't bother him. He needs to focus all his energy on that. You have to help me. Now the water's starting to come into the den. It's going to flood the whole house. I know it. It's going to ruin all the furniture. What should I do?"

"First of all, you need to shut off the water. Get a screwdriver and a wrench. The box to shut off the water is in front of the house by the sidewalk. Use the screwdriver to take the lid off the water box. Then use the wrench to turn the brass knob—"

"I can't do that." Andrea's voice skipped up another level in pitch. Stacy guessed one notch from hysterical. "I don't know where the tools are or what a wrench looks like. I need someone to help me. You've got to do something!"

How could any person be so helpless?

"Mother, there's nothing I can do from here in Colorado."

"Don't yell at me!"

She wasn't yelling. Her mom always accused Stacy of that when she didn't do exactly what Andrea wanted or became the least bit forceful. Stacy counted to ten and vowed to keep her voice emotionless. "Ask one of the neighbors to help you shut off the water. If you can't find one of them, call the plumber. Tell him you can't shut off the water and you need him to come to the house as soon as possible."

She refused to think about what an emergency "drop everything and come right now" fee would be as Colt returned. "I've got to go."

"I don't know where the plumber's number is."

"I'll send it to you." Then she ended the call before her mother could ask her to call the plumber for her. After she texted the phone number to Andrea, she turned off her phone's ringer and shoved it in her back pocket.

"Problems?" Colt asked.

Just the same old, same old. My mother can't cope with the smallest problems and wants me to take care of everything.

"My mom's got water all over the garage, and expects me to fix everything for her from here."

"All she needs to do is shut off the water and call a plumber."

"That's what I told her, but from the way she reacted you'd think I asked her to build a nuclear reactor." Stacy rubbed her temples in an attempt to ease her pounding headache.

Her phone vibrated in her pocket. Her mother would have deal with the problem on her own.

"Your butt's buzzing."

"I know. At least I'll get a good minimassage from all her calls."

"You aren't going to answer?"

Guilt tickled her conscience. She could give the plumber a quick call, but then irritation kicked in. Her mother could make a simple phone call and deal with the plumber. "No, I'm not going to talk to her right now."

"Good for you. Sometimes you have to be tough. If I did everything for my daughter she'd never learn to stand on her own. Sounds like your mom needs to deal with the water problem or learn to swim."

His validating words lifted the brick off her chest. She wasn't being the worst daughter ever by expecting her mother to deal with this problem. "You're absolutely right. Thank you." Her phone vibrated again. "What's next on the training schedule?"

"Now comes the big test. We're going into the stall. I'll get Babe bridled and then you'll lead her to the arena."

Her stomach plummeted. "You said all I'd have to do was walk beside and help Ryan."

"Which means you will actually *have to stand beside* the horse." He started to walk toward the stall, then stopped and glanced over his shoulder at her. She couldn't move.

"You want me to go in a closed space with a horse?"

His gaze softened as he returned to her. When he stopped in front of her she couldn't breathe. The confidence in his eyes reached out to her. Confidence in her, but not in the way Andrea looked at her as though she'd do whatever needed to be done. The look in Colt's eyes was different. He believed in *her*.

"Trust me. I won't let anything happen to you."

This time when he headed toward Babe's stall, she followed. Once inside, she scooted to a corner as far away from the pony as possible.

"You stay there until you feel comfortable. There's nothing to worry about. Babe's a sweet girl." He patted the animal's neck. "I can't believe you're starring in a movie about women who own a horse ranch. Won't your fear of horses be a problem?"

"I was worried about that until I read the script. My character doesn't have any scenes where she needs to ride. Of course things can change, but when I auditioned for the role, I told Maggie about my issues. She said she didn't think it would be a problem, but if it was, we'd work through it."

"That's another reason why you need to get more comfortable around horses. Your character will be more believable if you don't break into a cold sweat when a horse is within ten feet of you."

"I'm not sweating."

"Liar."

"You're such a gentleman."

"Have you forgotten about how I came to your defense at Halligan's?"

"That was then. This is now."

He nodded toward her and smiled. "That's better. See, you're almost next to Babe and you're still breathing."

She hadn't realized that as they'd talked, she'd moved closer to him, and thus, to the horse. The man could make a nun feel comfortable in a strip club.

He slipped the bridle on as he explained important things she needed to know about horses. Never stand directly behind one. Don't duck under the animal's neck. Go around him so he's not startled. "The best place to stand is by the horse's shoulder where you both can see each other."

She started to relax. The horse seemed pretty calm.

"When you're leading a horse, make sure *you're* the leader. You move first. The horse follows you." Then he held out a rope to her. "Here's the keys."

She wasn't sure she was ready for this, but if she couldn't get near a horse, she couldn't be part of Ryan's therapy. Needing Colt's reassurance that she could do this, her gaze sought his.

"Trust me. I won't let anything happen to you."

Her heart tripped. Heaven help her, but she believed him. That's the kind of man he was. When he gave his word, it meant something. Not like most of the people in her life. In her life? She had a handful of friends, but would they be there for her if she asked? More like she had close colleagues, and in her business, a promise meant something could be counted on unless things changed or a better deal came along.

Hand shaking, she took the rope from him. "What do I do now?"

"Start walking to the stall door. She'll follow."

You can do this. Don't let fear rule you.

Muttering the phrases like a mantra, she started walking. The pony fell in step behind her.

"You're doing great."

Colt kept offering encouragement, and she made it through the stall door. As they walked down the hallway to the arena, the pony's hooves clicked on the cement floor like a drumbeat. A sense of accomplishment bolted through her as they left the barn and entered the arena. Her breath came out in a soft rush. She glanced at Colt. "I did it."

"You sure did." The pride in his eyes drilled into her. The man made her feel as if she could do anything.

For the next hour they worked together. She led Babe around the arena and Colt gave instructions as he would during a therapy session. They talked about various situations that could come up.

"I'm feeling comfortable with Babe, but what about Chance? He's so huge."

"We screen our horses and they go through training, too. People don't realize, only one out of fifteen horses works for a program like this. What I'm trying to say is, the animals in my program are the safest horses a person can be around."

She'd take his word for it.

As they walked back to the barn, Colt said, "If you really want to understand what Ryan's going through and get over your fear, you should get on a horse. You'd realize what great animals they are." He opened the arena gate for her to lead Babe through. "You and I could go riding some day."

"Riding?"

"More like walking through the national park like the tourists do. We could make an afternoon of it. Stop along the way and have a picnic."

She froze. As if him asking her to go riding hadn't thrown her enough, he'd gone on to explain. He couldn't be doing what she thought he was doing. She knew that, but had to ask. "Are you asking me out on a date?"

Chapter 8

Colt hadn't meant to ask Stacy out. The words asking her to go riding jumped out before he considered what he was saying. He almost winced. Obviously he'd botched the invitation, since she wasn't sure he'd asked her out, but now that he had, maybe it wasn't such a bad thing.

He'd been strung tighter than a barbed wire fence since he'd kissed her. Hell, since they'd met he found himself thinking about her at the oddest times—sitting in the carpool lane waiting to pick Jess up or while he tried to write grant proposals. The fantasies were getting so bad this morning he'd taken a cold shower to get his body under control.

He needed to get her out of his system. If he spent time with her, got to know her, he'd see she wasn't any different than he expected—a fancy city woman. He'd see she'd never be happy in his life. He'd see how much her career meant to her and how much she loved California. Then she'd quit driving him insane. He would be able to stop dreaming about her. He'd quit imagining what it would be like to make love to her.

"I don't think us going out would be a good idea."

From the look of almost horror splashed across her face now, he wished he could take back what he'd said. In an effort to salvage his tattered pride he said, "Did you hear me mention the word *date?*"

"No."

"I offered to help you get over your fear so you could understand your brother's therapy better and because it would help you do a better job in your movie. Think of it as research." He couldn't believe he'd said those words with a straight face. God ought to be striking him with lightning for that whopper.

"Since my character doesn't need to ride a horse or even sit on one in this movie, I think I can call it good with what I've done today."

"Not even if I put you on a horse that's so

old she couldn't do more than walk if I lit a fire under her? It can't get much safer than that."

"I'll pass."

"Chicken?"

"Absolutely. The closest I'm getting to a horse is being Ryan's sidewalker."

That was probably for the best. He'd finish her training. They'd see each other around town and at Ryan's therapy. Fine with him.

That night Colt sat at the kitchen table with Jess and tried to find the words to talk to her about what she'd confided in Stacy earlier. Damn, parenting was hard work and seemed to get more difficult as she grew up. He'd thought figuring out why she was crying as a baby was tough? That didn't come close to talking to her about sex, dating and her mother running off on them. They'd discussed her mother leaving before, but when Jess said she was fine and understood her mother leaving wasn't her fault, he left things at that.

Because he hadn't really wanted to deal with the truth and her pain. Or his. But he couldn't do that any longer.

Never one to go around the fence when he could open the gate, he decided on the direct approach. "I heard what you said to Stacy about the last conversation you had with your mom. Why didn't you tell me about it?"

"You were eavesdropping?"

"No. I came into the barn to meet her for our training session and heard you talking. I was going to let you know I was there, but then I heard what she said and stopped. She said pretty much what I would've. I figured you needed to hear that from someone else. Your mom knew you loved her. If she were here, she'd tell you she knew you didn't mean what you said. She wouldn't want you feeling guilty over it."

"You really think so?"

"Absolutely."

"I was so mad at her, and I never got the chance to take back what I said."

"Stacy was right. You've got to let it go."

"Why did she have to leave town? If she'd stayed here…"

Jess's words trailed off, but he knew what his daughter had been about to say. *If she'd stayed here she would still be alive.*

If he'd said Lynn could come back that day she might still be alive, too, but that's something he'd have to live with. He wouldn't burden his daughter with that. "I'll be honest. I think she was searching for something and she didn't think she could find it here." His hand covered his daughter's smaller one. She laced her fingers with his and held on so tight his fingers started to go numb. "I don't want you thinking it was your fault she left."

Lynn wanted the freedom she'd have had if she hadn't gotten married so young and had a baby right away.

He never felt as if their decision caused him to miss out on life. He'd already decided to go into the Air Force and getting married didn't change that. Lynn had felt differently. She'd planned on going to college. When she tried attending later when Jess was a toddler, juggling motherhood, classes and studying with a husband who wasn't always around proved too much for her. He'd mentioned her trying again a few years later when Jess went to elementary school, but Lynn hadn't been interested.

"Your mom left me. I truly believe when she was more settled, she'd have asked you to live with her if you'd wanted to." He wasn't really sure about that, but his daughter needed to hear the words, and he figured God would forgive him for that lie. "Then you would've had the opportunity to tell her you didn't mean what you'd said. Fate took that chance away from you."

"I miss her so much some times, especially when I hear friends talking about all the stuff they do with their moms."

Nothing he could do could ever change that. There were events in a girl's life she wanted to share with her mother—picking out a prom dress, planning a wedding, the birth of her first child—and Jess would have to navigate those milestones without her mother's guidance. He recalled Reed telling him while he was in Afghanistan how he'd taken Jess shopping for a dress for the Spring Fling. The experience still gave his brother nightmares, and he'd been forced to call Avery in as a reinforcement. That's the best Jess would ever have—stand-ins for her mom.

That's what angered him most about Lynn's leaving, what she'd left her daughter alone to deal with.

"I wish I could tell you that will get easier, but I'm not sure it will. Things will happen in your life, and you'll wish your mom was there to share them with you."

"I'm just so glad I have you."

"But it's not the same," he said. "When you're missing your mom, it's okay to talk to me about it."

"I know it hurts you to talk about her."

He'd tried to keep his daughter from seeing

how much, but apparently he hadn't done as good a job as he thought. "I don't need you to protect me. It's not your job. I loved your mom. She was a big part of my life. We had some wonderful times together and the best thing we ever did was create you. I don't want to erase that part of my life. Got it?"

He needed to let go, too. Of his anger at Lynn for leaving him with such an awful mess to clean up. Of his guilt for the fact that she'd been so unhappy with him she'd felt the need to leave town and had gotten herself killed. Of his grief over the death of the love of his youth.

"Now since we're talking about you feeling the need to protect me, what were you thinking when you asked Stacy what was going on between her and I?"

"You haven't dated in forever."

When she emphasized the last word he cringed. "That's right. Dinosaurs roamed the Earth when your mom and I were dating."

"You're a great guy, but Stacy's used to Hollywood actors."

Ouch. When his daughter thought he couldn't compete with the guys Stacy normally dated that really hurt. "While I get to get to give your dates the third degree, you are to stay out of my love life."

"What love—"

"Don't even say it."

He didn't need to hear his fifteen-year-old daughter say he didn't have a love life. He knew the fact all too well.

Despite the success of her training session a few days earlier, Stacy's nerves started getting the best of her as she drove to Healing Horses.

"You don't have to do this, you know," Ryan said, his face etched with concern for her.

She released her death grip on the steering wheel and flashed him a tight smile. "I want to."

"No, you don't. I can tell because that's your too-big smile again."

"You're seriously making me doubt my skills as an actress." He was right. She hadn't wanted to, but that wasn't the only thing she was nervous about. She wasn't sure how to deal with Colt now. Ever since he'd kissed her she didn't know what was going on between them, and the other day only ratcheted up the attraction between them.

"You're great on a movie set, but not so hot at hiding your feelings in real life."

"I want to be there for your therapy sessions."

"You mean in a way other than from the opposite side of the fence or hanging over Colt's shoulder?"

She glared at her brother. "You're never going to let me forget that, are you?"

Ryan laughed. "You've got to admit it. That was funny when he picked you up. You should have seen the look on your face. Talk about looking weirded out."

"It wasn't so hilarious from my perspective." Being in Colt's arms brought a variety of emotions to life along with her outrage—excitement, desire, longing. A whole lot of longing. The feelings had only grown stronger when they worked together the other day. If he hadn't looked at her with such confidence it would've been easier to stay detached. If he hadn't been so patient and so damned understanding. Dealing with him as the overbearing, take-charge Neanderthal man was much simpler. And safer.

She cleared her throat and turned to Ryan. "I think this will be good for me. In an odd way, the training and dealing with my fear of horses is helping me deal with Dad's death."

More than the years of therapy ever had. Little bits and pieces of the days before her dad's accident had started coming back to her. Snippets of conversations between the director and her father about whether or not he should let a stuntman do the scene. Her dad had argued that he could handle the stunt. The director had expressed his concern, and her dad had countered with the realism would enhance his performance.

"It had to be tough being there when Dad died. I wish I'd gotten to know him."

Over the years she'd tried to share her memories of their father with Ryan, but it wasn't the same as him having his own. As she turned into the Healing Horses driveway, she said, "You're a lot like him, and not just in looks. You've got his easy way with people, his charm. You've got his good heart."

At least before the accident squelched that wonderful part of Ryan's personality. Since they'd arrived in Colorado, she'd seen sparks of that person returning.

As she parked her car, her stomach tightened. What had Colt said? *Courage isn't the absence of fear, but the mastery of it.*

She kept telling herself that as they prepared for Ryan's therapy. When she and Ryan stood on the mounting block as Colt led Chance in, her heart pounded almost painfully as the large animal approached. Colt's gaze locked with hers. The confidence in her she'd seen there the other day blazed there now. *He believes in me. He thinks I can do this.*

Her courage bolstered, she fought down her urge to run. Colt's words rang in her ears. *The animals in my program are the safest horses a person can be around.* Chance didn't even glance her way as Colt and the animal stood in front of them. "You okay?"

She nodded, too afraid to say anything.

While he stood by the horse's head, Colt said, "Stacy, help Ryan get his foot in the stirrup. His upper body is strong. He can take it from there."

She nodded again, but said nothing, not wanting to do anything to confuse Chance. Once Ryan was mounted, Colt led Chance forward, away from the mounting area and headed toward the arena. From her training she knew her job was to walk beside the horse. She wouldn't need to do anything other than to watch for Ryan having balancing problems. If that occurred, she was to place her hand on his boot near his ankle. That would offer him extra stability. If that wasn't enough she could move her arms across his thigh and grasp the front edge of the saddle.

For the next hour she walked beside her

brother. The slight changes in his control and balance as they progressed through the session amazed her. After working in the arena for a while, they stopped by an area containing what looked like a bean bag game kids might play at a birthday party.

Colt handed Ryan bean bags and told him which hole in the board to aim for. Ryan had to work on maintaining control of Chance as he threw bags at the target. Though he struggled with keeping Chance still on his first attempts, Colt offered suggestions and Ryan quickly improved. When a bean bag finally sailed through the designated spot, Stacy bit her lip to keep from cheering. Not only because of her brother's accomplishment, but from the pride shining on his face.

If only Andrea could see what a different this therapy was making for Ryan.

You can't get blood out of a turnip. Or manufacture love where the capacity for the emotion didn't exist. Sure, Andrea had been married three times, but the desperate need to be taken care of, not real love, fueled her actions.

The thought barreled through Stacy. Had she ever been in love? Maybe like her mother she didn't possess the ability to truly love that way.

No, she loved Ryan. But what about loving a man? She shook herself mentally and focused her attention to Ryan through the remainder of the session. When they returned to the barn, Jess met them. She smiled at Ryan. "You're doing great. You must've been a cowboy in a past life."

"Thanks. You want to help me groom Chance?"

Once Ryan dismounted, he and Jess led Chance back to his stall and Stacy couldn't contain her excitement any longer. "I did it, Colt. I walked beside that huge horse, and eventually I wasn't so scared."

"I'm shocked that you were able to be quiet for that long."

"Do you overwhelm all your volunteers with this much gratitude and praise? Would it be so hard to toss me a bone? To say I did a good job?"

He shifted his stance, his scuffed cowboy boots kicked up dust with his movements. "You did a damned fine job. I'm duly impressed."

His words thrilled her as much as an Academy Award nomination would.

"I could tell how hard it was for you to keep quiet, especially when Ryan hit the right spot in the target that first time."

"That was pretty cool," Ryan said as he and Jess returned.

She glanced at Jess and then at Colt. "How about it? You two want to go out to dinner celebrate our success—Ryan's improvement and my first session as a sidewalker? My treat."

"We've got plans. We're having dinner at my brother's house tonight," Colt replied.

"I bet Uncle Reed and Aunt Avery wouldn't mind if Stacy and Ryan came, too," Jess added.

"No, that's all right," Stacy murmured. "We can do it some other time."

But Jess wasn't listening. She'd already pulled out her cell phone and dialed.

"You wouldn't mind if my friend Ryan—the guy who came with me to volunteer at the shelter the other day—and his sister came to dinner with us tonight, would you?" Jess rattled on about Stacy being afraid of horses and how her dad talked her into becoming a sidewalker. "Ryan's therapy's going great, and Stacy survived her first time volunteering, so she asked us to celebrate."

Stacy cringed. Somehow when Jess said it that way, Stacy felt pathetic and alone. As if she had no one to share good news with other than Colt and his daughter.

And you think you do?

A minute later, Jess ended her call and Stacy said, "I appreciate you wanting to include us, Jess, but you have to call your aunt back. We're not going to horn in on a family event. We can celebrate some other time."

"It's cool. Aunt Avery said she's been meaning to ask you and Ryan over. She said you two met when you were here before."

Stacy cringed. She hadn't made the best impression with Griffin's family. She'd been a stuck-up pain in the ass, who hadn't cared about anything but advancing her career.

"Thank you, but no." She might be pathetic, but she still had some pride.

"If Jess's aunt is okay with it, what's the big deal?" Ryan asked.

"We weren't invited."

Then Jess and Ryan started talking at once trying to convince her to change her mind. When she remained adamant, Ryan said he didn't care what she did, but he was going.

A shrill whistle cut through the chatter. She and the teenagers turned to Colt, who stood there, feet braced, arms crossed over his broad chest in full take-charge mode. "We'll pick you up at seven." When Stacy started to protest, he held up a hand and stepped closer. The man had a presence that could make a girl swoon. "Don't make me throw you over my shoulder to get you there."

Stacy pointed her chin at him in defiance. "I won't let you in the house."

"I will," Ryan tossed out.

"Traitor," she snapped at him, without taking her gaze off Colt. "You wouldn't do that again."

"Wanna bet?"

No. She knew she'd lose. "We'll see you at seven."

By six forty-five Stacy considered telling Ryan she was coming down with a cold, the flu, the plague or whatever other disease she could think of to avoid going to dinner. She'd changed her clothes three times. Everything she owned seemed so—California Hollywood. After her last meeting with Avery and the incident at Halligan's she didn't want to look as if she was putting on airs.

The first time she'd stayed in Estes Park she'd been so concerned about her career and looking good for the cameras that she never treated anyone like... She paused. She hadn't really given anyone here much thought, but things were different now.

Because of Colt. She didn't want to embarrass him tonight with his family.

Settling on a simple cobalt knit top and jeans, she added her favorite chunky silver necklace and earrings and glanced in the mirror. *I'm as ready as I'll ever be.*

When she answered the door after the doorbell rang a couple of minutes before seven, her breath caught in her throat. There stood Colt looking way too fine in dark jeans and a tan shirt that highlighted his golden skin and hair.

His heated gaze scanned her from head to toe. The appreciative male grin that he flashed her bolstered her courage. A pleasant flush spread through her. "You look great, Stacy."

"So do you."

Lord this was awkward. *That's because it feels like a date.*

Anxious to blast that thought out of her mind, she called out, "Ryan, hurry up. Colt's here."

Footsteps pounded overhead and then down the stairs. A minute later, the three of them headed out the door. Once in the car, Ryan and Jess talked nonstop in the backseat. Unable to stand the silence between her and Colt any longer she asked, "How long have your brother and Avery been married?"

"Since early December, but they've known

each other their whole lives. They were high school sweethearts until Reed left for Stanford." Colt told her how his brother came from California to stay with Jess when he'd been deployed. "Jess got sentenced to community service at Avery's animal shelter for vandalism—"

"In my defense, I didn't actually participate in the spray painting," Jess explained. "Some friends of mine, who're no longer my friends, I might add, did the vandalism. Then they ran off and left me to take the fall."

Now Jess taking Ryan under her wing made more sense. Her mother ran off, then died. Her father was deployed to Afghanistan, and her friends bailed on her leaving her to take the rap for their vandalism. Yup, the girl understood what it felt like to be on the outside.

"The good news was," Jess continued, "because of a shelter policy, Uncle Reed had to volunteer with me. That's how he and Avery got back together."

Family. Jess's affection for her uncle and his wife rippled through her voice.

Colt, his daughter and brother obviously had the give and take true families possessed. When Stacy visited Estes Park before, she'd envied Griffin's relationship with his family.

He had a home filled with love and people who supported him. When he defied the network and proposed to Maggie on the finale, his family and the community rallied around him. They hadn't left him standing alone to fight the battle. Now, since Colt's brother had married Avery McAlister, he and Jess had been enveloped in the McAlister clan, as well.

As they walked from the parking lot to Avery and Reed's apartment, Stacy tried to quell her nervousness. What was the big deal? It was just a simple dinner at someone's house. At someone's house that she hadn't made the best first impression on.

When Avery answered the door, Stacy was amazed at how the woman, with only a bit of lip gloss and mascara, dressed in scrubs and scuffed tennis shoes, could look as though she belonged on the cover of a magazine. "Come on in. I just got home. We had some abandoned kittens come in to the shelter right before I left. We couldn't find their mother, so I get to spend the night feeding them every two hours."

"Sounds like fun," Colt joked.

"The joys of having a wife who brings her work home." A tall, dark-haired man and the scraggliest dog Stacy had ever seen tagging after him joined them. The man wrapped his arms around Avery, and then introduced himself as Colt's brother.

She'd never guess they were related, much less brothers. Except for their height, Colt and Reed Montgomery had nothing in common physically.

"Do you need any help with the kittens?" Jess asked. "If you do, I could spend the night and help out."

"You can help me with their next feeding before you leave," Avery said.

"Reed, the timer went off, so I took the lasagna out of the oven." Nannette McAlister strolled out of the kitchen. "Everything's on the table so we're ready to eat."

Griffin's mother was here? Now Stacy wished she'd pulled the "I'm sick" routine. When she'd met Nannette, the older woman made no secret of the fact that not only didn't she approve of her son going on the reality dating show, she didn't think much of the bachelorettes, either.

Could this night get any worse?

In a lame attempt to ease the tension she felt, Stacy said, "Thank you for letting us join you. I hope it hasn't caused too much trouble." Her words sounded as awkward as she felt. She nodded toward Mrs. McAlister. "It's good to see you again."

The older woman nodded and mumbled a polite greeting in return. As everyone moved into the small dining room conversations swirled around Stacy. Once Ryan sat, she took his walker, pushed it into the nearby corner and then settled into her chair in between him and Colt. She felt herself pulling inward as she tried to come up with an excuse to leave once they finished eating. Coming from a small family who never ate dinner together, sitting down with a total of seven people overwhelmed her.

"Your adventures at Halligan's the other night are the talk of the town, big brother. Did you really get into a bar fight with Travis Carpenter?"

Stacy cringed. The night just got worse.

Chapter 9

Colt wanted to jump across the table and punch his brother. Didn't Reed realize how uncomfortable this conversation would make Stacy feel?

Since they arrived, Stacy had changed. Instead of the fearless, say-what's-on-her-mind woman he knew, she'd become quiet. Almost as if she wanted to blend in with the furniture.

Now his jackass brother brought up the night at Halligan's. Beside him he almost felt Stacy pulling away even further. He didn't know where she'd gone, but she wasn't here with them. At least not the feisty woman he knew.

"Thanks for bringing that up, Reed, because I haven't been embarrassed enough by everyone in town asking me about the fight."

His brother flashed him a stupid grin. "Glad to help out. What happened? Getting into a bar fight isn't your style."

Before he could answer, Jess spoke, her young face scrunched up with revulsion. "You should've seen it. Mr. Carpenter's hands were all over Stacy."

"We don't need to rehash all the gory details," Colt said, hoping everyone would take the hint and move on to another topic.

"So you played the knight in shining armor coming to a lady's rescue. Now that seems like you," Reed said.

Yeah, he was a regular white knight. One who charged in before he thought about the consequences or the fact that his daughter was watching.

Out of the corner of his eye he spotted Stacy, her posture all rigid, her back looking as if it had been glued to the chair. "Anyone see the Rockies game yesterday? Looks like they might have a good season this year."

"What Carpenter was doing must have been bad because Colt's the kind of guy who follows the rules no matter what. Nothing riles him. He's got more patience than anyone I know," Avery said, ignoring his obvious attempt to change the subject. Getting this group to move on to a different subject would be as easy as a getting a bull out of a pasture full of cows.

"How awful for you, Stacy."

Stacy's eyes widened as if she couldn't believe someone was talking to her. "The man had more arms than an octopus. It might not have been so bad if he hadn't been drunk."

"It's about time someone knocked some sense into that man," Nannette added. "Travis always has been too big for his britches. That's his father's fault. Travis is the youngest. He's got four older sisters. His father was so glad to finally have a boy he treated his son like his diapers didn't stink."

Reed laughed. "He'd sure be different if he'd had a mother like you."

"You're right about that. Mom never tolerated any of us putting on airs," Avery said. "I'd heard when Travis drinks his manners evaporate."

"That's a nice way to put it," Stacy said, her body relaxing some as the topic moved away from their actions at the bar, focusing on Carpenter instead. "Travis wouldn't let me leave the dance floor."

Nannette gaze filled with compassion and concern when she turned to Stacy. "How frightening. Thank goodness Colt was there to step in."

"And what thanks did he get? He got hauled off to jail." Stacy turned to him, and the fire blazing in her clear blue eyes told Colt the feisty woman he knew had returned.

"It turned out okay. Having to listen to a lecture from Chief Parsons was the worst part. Other than that, I had to pay a fine and for part of the damages at Halligan's."

"That's not fair. You didn't start the fight," Ryan said.

"I'll talk to Chief Parsons. You did nothing wrong." Stacy shook her head. "I knew I should've contacted my attorney that night. If I had this wouldn't have happened."

"It's no big deal." He wanted to forget the night ever happened, and not only because of the fight. "As far as I'm concerned the matter's over."

"I'll reimburse you for the fine and whatever the damages were."

"It's already taken care of." He didn't need her seeing to his responsibilities. He'd gotten into the fight. He'd man up and take the consequences.

"That's the least I can do since you were defending me."

"There's no need."

"I don't want what happened taking money away from Healing Horses or from other necessities. It's not easy surviving on one income."

He winced. What did she think? That he was a charity case? "I do all right."

"I didn't say you weren't. At least let me pay half."

"No."

"Why won't you let me help you?"

Her words stopped him cold, her offer both thrilling and ticking him off. Anger kicked in both at her for wanting to help and at him for being pleased that she had. "I don't need the help."

"Is Healing Horses having money problems?" Reed's voice startled Colt. He pulled his gaze away from Stacy.

Five sets of eyes trained on him and Stacy.

He'd forgotten everyone else. For a few minutes there had been no one around but Stacy. The woman made him lose all common sense. She lit a fire in him like no other woman. Not even his wife. No woman ever made him so out-and-out frustrated, or made him want her so much.

After a deep breath and counting to ten, he said, "Healing Horses is doing fine. The spring classes are full. We just got another grant. If I get real lucky at an auction I should be able to pick up a few more horses."

"I'm going to one this weekend," Avery said. "We received an anonymous donation to purchase horses to keep them from going to meat packers."

"What?" Stacy and Ryan gasped in unison.

"Horse meat is a delicacy in some places in Europe. Meat packers will buy unwanted horses here and ship the meat overseas."

"How can people do that?" Ryan's voice filled with horror. "Horses are such beautiful animals."

"I know. With the donation we'll buy as many horses as we can. Then we'll find adoptive homes for them."

"I never knew this kind of thing happened. How awful." Stacy glanced at Avery. "How can I help? Can I make a donation to the shelter?"

"I'll always take money, or you could come with us to the auction and bid on horses yourself. If you, Colt and I all bid that would help keep the prices up and knock out a lot of the meat packers. They want to get the horses dirt cheap."

"I should update the website to let people know how they can help, and that the shelter will have horses available for adoption," Reed said.

"I'll send out something on Facebook," Jess added. "Ryan, you can help me with that. I'll also do a blog on the subject for the shelter."

They thankfully spent the rest of the meal discussing Healing Horses, Avery's work at the shelter and Reed's business. All safe topics. Stacy opened up and talked about Maggie's movie and her role. "People are calling the movie a female *Bonanza* for the twenty-first century. If it does well at the box office, who knows, it could lead to a series."

"I think Maggie's movie will be a blockbuster. Everybody's always talking about how great cowboys are, how they're the backbone of the West and all that kind of stuff, but nobody ever shows how strong the women are here," Jess said.

Avery nodded toward her mom. "Look at Mom. She's a perfect example of that."

"I've had a lot of help running my ranch from my kids." Nannette, beaming from her daughter's compliment, turned toward Stacy. "I know you've done both movies and series. Which do you prefer, Stacy?"

"Movies are great, but a series means getting to stay in one place and money coming in consistently. Those things have a big appeal now that Ryan's living with me."

"That's what Maggie says. She and Griffin love doing *The Next Rodeo Cowboy,* but once my granddaughter is school age, they don't want to do all that traveling."

"Then we'll have to hope the movie is a huge success, and Maggie gets the chance to direct the series," Avery said.

"They could film it here," Reed added. "Now that would be a boost to the local economy."

After dinner, Jess and Ryan took Avery's laptop and went to the living room to work on getting the word out about the auction on social media. When Avery and Nannette started clearing the table, Stacy picked up her plate and Colt's. Then he picked up some glasses.

"While I appreciate your willingness to help, Colt, my kitchen's not that big," Avery said. "And if you help clean up, then Reed will feel like he has to help. Then we'll be tripping over each other like puppies trying to get to their mom at feeding time."

"She's right," Reed said. "You can help me update the website."

Colt glanced at Stacy, trying to sense if she felt comfortable being left alone. Then he shook himself mentally. What was he worried about? This was Nannette and Avery.

"Go," Stacy said, as if reading his mind. How did she do that?

As he and Reed walked through the apartment to his brother's office, Reed asked, "Are things really okay with Healing Horses? If you need money, RJ Industries can give you another grant."

"I don't need my baby brother bailing me out."

"Think of it as me paying you back for helping me reach adulthood. Hell, if it hadn't been for you either Dad would've killed me, or I'd be in jail for killing him."

When his brother settled in at his desk, Colt sank into the wing chair in the corner of the room. "Damn, Reed. Getting into that fight with Carpenter scared the daylights out of me. With our history and the way Dad was—"

"You are nothing like that bastard."

"You didn't see me at Halligan's. I'm not sure I've ever been that mad."

"He started the fight. You didn't go out looking for one. Remember how our old man used to do that?" Anger filled Reed's gaze, but the emotion was different now. No, it wasn't exactly anger. More regret and resignation. "Some days I would look at him and know it was going to be a rough one. The look that he was spoiling for a fight was in his eyes. We're not like that."

Certainty rang out in Reed's voice, and Colt knew he was right. Despite his fight with Carpenter, he wasn't like his father. That didn't mean the feelings Stacy stirred up in him that night didn't leave him shaking in his boots. "Thanks. I needed to hear that. How did we turn out okay when he was such a dick?"

"I had you and the McAlisters' house to escape to. You had Lynn."

Wow. The words knocked Colt harder than an angry bull. Sure, he'd loved his wife, but had part of her allure been her family? Its stability, the calm that radiated her household? Lynn's house became his shelter amid the storm of his life. Had he used Lynn as an escape? Had that been another reason why they didn't make it?

What did it matter now? No use in feeling guilty when he couldn't change anything.

"Dinner was interesting. Stacy really gets under your skin." Reed pulled up the shelter's website. "I wondered what was going on between you two when I heard about what happened at Halligan's. I've never seen a woman light a fire under you like Stacy did when the two of you were arguing about her paying your fine. Not even Lynn got you that riled up."

His brother didn't know the half of it. Not that Colt planned on admitting the fact.

Play dumb.

"There's nothing between me and Stacy."

Reed laughed, and not just a little chuckle. No. A full out belly laugh. "How could you say that with a straight face?'"

Discipline learned from years in the military.

But he couldn't deny it. Stacy annoyed him more than any woman he'd ever met, and yet he admired her. Her spunk, her fortitude. The courage it took her to get anywhere near a horse after one killed her father. He liked how she spoke her mind. He thought of their earlier discussion tonight. No doubt about it, a man knew what she was thinking because she held nothing in.

Lynn had been the opposite. She never said what she thought, preferring instead to let him guess. Usually wrong. No, she held everything in and then one day she'd blast him out of the water with how mad she was. That's what happened with their marriage. He'd sensed for a while that she was unhappy and brought up the subject a couple of times.

She smiled and said nothing was wrong. He'd known better, but hadn't wanted to push. To tell the truth, he hadn't wanted to know how bad things were. Then one day she waltzed in, said she'd been miserable for years and left. No talking about it. No giving him a chance to change. She'd given up on him.

He couldn't see Stacy giving up on anything or anyone.

"I think it's great that you're interested in a woman. It's about time you came back among the living male population."

He stared at Reed. "What's that supposed to mean?"

"You've been a monk since Lynn left. Is that what you really want? To spend the rest of your life alone?"

The last thing Colt needed was someone else to worry about, and that's what happened with relationships. All he wanted was a calm, boring life, without any further entanglements. He needed a romantic relationship like a farmer needed to milk a bull. Plus he had Jess to consider. He couldn't risk bringing someone into her life who might leave her. She'd dealt with so much in her life. She couldn't handle any more loss and Stacy would leave.

"I'm happy for you and Avery, but I'm already a onetime loser. That was enough for me. Only an idiot with a track record like mine would go there again."

"Who said anything about marriage? Go out on a date."

"I'm not sure I remember what to do. I only dated one girl before I started dating Lynn and that was when I was sixteen."

"Suffering from performance anxiety?"

After the other night? No way. His body remembered exactly how to react to a woman and what to do with one. That was the problem.

"Things have changed a whole helluva lot since then," he said.

"Just go out and have some fun. Go to dinner. A movie, whatever. Anything but taking her to a family dinner." Reed shook his head. "What were you thinking?"

"It wasn't my idea. It was my daughter's."

How did a guy just date and have fun? If there wasn't any chemistry with a woman he might as well go out with his buddies instead. If there was a spark between them, then how did he keep from wanting more? No thanks. Dating sounded like a recipe for disaster.

"I don't know why we're talking about this. Stacy'sonly going to be around for a few weeks. Once her brother's done with therapy and she finishes the movie she'll hightail it back to L.A."

"That's perfect. You can have a good time with both of you knowing nothing else can come of it. That's a great way for you to get your feet wet."

"What about Jess? She got attached to Avery pretty quick when you two started dating. What if she does the same with Stacy? I don't know if she could take getting close to Stacy and then having her leave."

"If you're worried about Jess dealing with it, talk with her."

"Talk with my teenage daughter about my dating a woman? That's just what I need."

"You're thinking too much. Jess knows Stacy isn't sticking around, right?" Colt nodded. "Then it shouldn't be a problem. Trust me on this. What harm could having a little fun do?"

Somehow Colt didn't think things would be that simple.

"You don't have to help clean up, Stacy," Avery said once Colt and Reed left. "You're a guest. Mom and I can handle it."

She didn't want to be a guest.

When she'd said how Travis wouldn't let her leave the dance floor, both women understood what she'd felt. Compassion had filled their eyes, and Nannette had shown a mother's concern. Would Andrea have cared if she knew what happened at Halligan's? Really cared about her and how scared she'd been? Something told Stacy all Andrea would've been more concerned about was how to turn what happened into a publicity op.

Her heart skipped a beat. She wanted to belong.

"Helping will give me a chance to apologize to both of you for the way I acted the last time I was in town," Stacy said as she followed the women into the kitchen.

"No hard feelings." Nannette carried plates to the sink. "Griffin was as much to blame for what happened on that show as anyone else."

"You're right about that," Avery added. "If he'd told Maggie he loved her before the finale, things would've been so much better."

"He wasn't ready to admit that then." Nannette turned to Stacy, a glint in her eye as if she were about to share a secret. "My children can be a little hardheaded."

"Mom, I'm right here."

"I know you are, dear." Nannette kissed her daughter on the cheek. "I love you, but you know I'm right."

Love filled the small kitchen as it had at

the dinner. Deep. Constant. Unfailing. Stacy looked away.

"I wasn't being hardheaded. I was being cautious with Reed." Avery pointed to the stove. "Would you hand me that pot, Stacy?"

She nodded and retrieved the item. "I'm glad things worked out for Griffin and Maggie. When I've seen them together on the set they seem very happy. Now that's the only way to find love on a reality show and have it last."

"I was right," Avery said, a huge grin on her face. "I never thought you were on that silly show expecting to find love."

"How anyone who watches that show can expect couples to stay together longer than the time it takes to boil water is beyond me," Nannette added.

"You'd be surprised how many people believe that's really why I went on the show." She explained about how she'd needed to revive her career.

"You've changed since you were here before," Avery said.

Lately, she felt as if that was a lifetime ago. "My life's different than it was then." When she'd met Avery and Nannette her career had been everything. Andrea's second husband had taken her to the cleaners, and she'd turned to retail therapy to cope. The money flew out faster than the Concord, and Andrea started having trouble paying her bills. Feeling the added financial pressure to supplement her mother's finances to keep a roof over Ryan's head, Stacy needed the steady income a series offered. Then Ryan had the accident and he moved in with her. Things like that changed a woman fast. "*I* was different then."

"What do you think of Colt?" Nannette asked as she wiped the kitchen counter.

What a complicated question.

No, it wasn't. The answer was simple. *He's wonderful. Honest, dependable and sexier than a man had a right to be.*

"He's a great father, and he's helping Ryan so much. The work he does at Healing Horses has amazed me. He's really making a difference in people's lives."

"That's not an answer to the question. I asked what *you* thought of *him*." Nannette's knowing gaze drilled into Stacy.

Too bad. That's my story, and I'm sticking to it.

"He's a good man. I was thankful he was there at Halligan's."

"He got that from his mother. She was a good woman." Nannette shook her head. "I still can't believe we didn't know what hell those boys went through after their mother died."

Avery explained how Colt and Reed's mother died after falling down the stairs when Colt was twelve. Before her death, their mother shielded her sons from her husband's temper and his fists as much as she could. "Reed told me Colt could let a lot of what their dad said and did slide, but Reed always argued with their father. That made things worse. Colt was the one who calmed the disagreements down or stepped in when things got really bad between Reed and his dad. Reed swears Colt kept the two of them from killing each other."

The strength of character it took to survive what life dumped on Colt astounded her. No wonder he protected Jess so fiercely, and no wonder he'd been so appalled by getting into a fight. An abusive father, an unfaithful wife, a tour in Afghanistan where who knows what horrors he'd witnessed, and none of that broke him. The fact that he still possessed a kindness, a gentleness, spoke of his nature, and now she understood why his eyes sometimes held the look of an old soul.

She'd started falling down a slippery slope with Colt. She couldn't help admire him, but she couldn't think about what it would be like to have a man of such strength, such courage in her life. She couldn't imagine him as a soft place to fall when life left her battered and bruised, because if she did, it would be so easy to fall in love with Colt.

And that she refused to do.

Chapter 10

After cleaning the kitchen everyone congregated in the living room where the teenagers had started playing video games with Colt and Reed watching.

"I hate to be the one to end the party, but I had an early-morning shoot today, and it's catching up with me."

Ryan and Jess paused their game and started complaining.

"Do we have to leave? It's Friday night…"

"It's only ten o'clock."

"To avoid an inevitable heated discussion or pulling rank, I'll take Stacy home," Colt said.

Then Nannette said she would drop the

teenagers off when she left. That settled, he and Stacy headed for the car.

After two minutes of silence in the car, Colt turned to her. "Did something happen in the kitchen?"

"We just talked girl talk while we cleaned up. Nothing major."

Nothing other than I realized how easily I could get attached to you and your family and had a mini panic attack.

Heady and dangerous stuff. The night had been eye-opening and exhausting. Being part of the Montgomery/McAlister clan had been overwhelming and wonderful, but now came time to face reality again. While she could enjoy belonging for the night, that was all she could have. She had a life and responsibilities. Ones that didn't mesh with life in Colorado.

"I'm sorry Reed brought up what happened at Halligan's. I know it made you uncomfortable. He was so busy getting his digs in at me, he didn't see that."

"I wish you'd let me pay for your fines."

"We closed that discussion."

No, he had. She decided not to push the issue. She could always make an anonymous donation to Healing Horses to balance the scales with him when her finances leveled out.

"You don't have to go to the auction."

"Ryan sounded so excited about going. I'd hate to disappoint him."

"Just because you don't go doesn't mean he can't tag along with me and Jess."

"I really shouldn't go. I haven't had a chance to learn the changes in my lines for tomorrow night's shoot." Who was she trying to convince, him or her? Tonight had taught her a lesson. Friendship with Colt wouldn't be easy. Or satisfying. It was like trying to eat half a cookie. The little taste only left her wanting the whole treat.

"I understand. Work has to come first. I'll have Jess text Ryan about picking him up. You'll have the day to yourself."

As she jumped out of Colt's truck she realized she'd made the sensible choice deciding not to attend the auction. No use pressing her face against the store window when she couldn't afford to buy anything. Doing that only made her ache for what she couldn't have, but if she'd made the right decision, how come she felt so lousy?

After the dinner at Avery and Reed's, Stacy flipped a switch inside her head. She refused to get attached to Colt and Jess.

Instead of chatting and joking with him before the session started, she helped Ryan prepare. At first Colt appeared confused by her reserved attitude and tried to tease her out of it. He tried so hard to get her to talk to him. He'd even gone so far as to ask her why she'd changed. She'd fobbed him off with a lame comment about having a lot on her mind. The wounded look in his soft gaze nearly did her in, but eventually he quit trying, and that left her feeling even worse. What had she expected? That he'd fling her over his shoulder, carry her off and demand she tell him what was going on?

Despite days of rain putting them behind schedule, Stacy was pleased with how the movie was going. Colt had been right. Becoming more comfortable around horses improved her performance. She felt more at ease and identified with her character better, resulting in what she felt was her best work.

Now to catch up and avoid added financial costs, Maggie lengthened their filming hours, leaving Stacy with little time for anything other than work and Ryan's therapy. That meant they didn't go into town much and helped her avoid running into Colt.

The only good thing to occur over the past few weeks was the amazing physical progress Ryan had made. His balance and control of his legs improved enough that for short periods of time he'd traded the walker for a cane. The hope was with continued horsemanship and physical therapy and a lot of hard work he could eventually get rid of the walker completely.

Remembering what she'd learned about Colt from Avery and Nannette strengthened her resolve to keep her promise to Jess. About keeping her and Colt's relationship on the friendship level, but oh, how the man invaded her dreams, and not in a friendship way.

This morning she woke up from a doozie. In this one instead of Jess interrupting them the night of the fight at Halligan's, she and Colt continued their romantic play. They explored each other's bodies until they both lay naked together on the couch. Just as he'd been about to enter her fevered flesh, Stacy woke up, disappointed and aching.

To top off her day, the shoot had run long, forcing her to call Colt to ask if they could push back Ryan's therapy a half an hour. After a lecture about this being her one free pass and she'd better not ask to reschedule again, he agreed. If she hurried, she'd have time to grab takeout for her and Ryan. They could sit, eat and catch up before they headed to Colt's. They hadn't done much of that lately.

"Stacy, I need to talk to you in my office before you leave," Maggie called out.

"Sure thing. I'll be there in a minute." So much for getting to sit and eat with Ryan before his therapy. She pulled out her phone and texted her brother to make some mac and cheese or something for his dinner because she was running way late.

Maggie and Griffin lived in a simple wood-and-brick, ranch-style house they'd just built on the far edge of Twin Creeks Ranch. When she'd settled into the wing chair across from Maggie's desk, the director slid script pages across the smooth walnut surface. "We've had to make some changes to the scene where Brandon's character notifies you that the bank is threatening to foreclose on his ranch."

Script changes happened all the time, but the director never called an actor into the office to discuss them unless the alterations were substantial, or she thought the actor would balk at the modifications.

Stacy's hands shook as she picked up the papers and scanned the sheets. Instead of informing her in the living room, they'd changed the scene to outdoors. She was to be working on the ranch, on a horse when her boyfriend rides up on a four-wheeler.

"I hate to do this to you, knowing what

happened to your dad, and especially since we talked about this before filming, but the scene has so much more impact this way."

Stacy nodded, her entire body numb as she tried to absorb the shock. Walking beside a horse to help Ryan in his therapy sessions was one thing. Crawling on top of one was something else entirely.

"If you absolutely can't get on a horse, we can use a stunt woman and editing can mix those shots with close-ups of you."

Stacy clasped her hands together in her lap to keep them still. She was being silly. All she had to do was sit on the horse and then dismount when she saw her boyfriend arriving. Simple, but her mind couldn't help but dredge up memories of the shoot with her father so long ago. Cannons blasted. Horses reared. Her father tumbled to the ground. She pinched her eyes shut and tried to shove aside her memories. An image of Colt smiling at her with pride when she'd accepted the lead rope from him came to her.

"I'd prefer not to do the scene that way, but if we have to we can." Maggie's calm voice pulled Stacy back.

Volunteering at Healing Horses had taught her she had nothing to fear. This was a different movie. This wouldn't be a battle scene with loud noises and gun blasts. She could do this.

"I'm willing to try, but can I ask for a couple of things?"

"Anything."

"Can we keep the crew to a minimum?"

Maggie nodded.

What else did she need to be able to pull this off?

Colt.

"I'd like Colt Montgomery to be there, and for him to pick the horse for me to ride. He trained me to be a volunteer in his therapy program." He wouldn't let anything happen to her. "I'd also like him to talk to the crew about what can make a horse skittish. That's why my dad died. The loud noises spooked the horse."

"I think that's a great idea. I can call Colt tonight."

No, she needed to ask him to do this. She needed to see in his eyes that he knew she could handle this. She needed his calm reassurance that he would keep her safe. "I'll see him in a little while at Ryan's therapy. I'll ask him."

"The plan is to shoot the scene on Saturday."

Stacy nodded. Today was Thursday. Part

of her wished she had more time to prepare, but then she'd only have more time to worry. Colt would make sure nothing went wrong.

If he agreed to help her. As she left Maggie's office and headed to her car Stacy nibbled on her lower lip. How could she ask him to do this for her when she'd all but ignored him lately? Especially when he'd looked at her so often with that old-soul look filling his gaze?

I hadn't wanted to hurt him, but I've done just that.

And now she planned on asking for his help. She'd be lucky if he'd even talk to her.

Ryan's therapy sessions had become torture for Colt. He'd missed Stacy. Talking with her. Joking around. Just being with her. He hadn't realized how much he looked forward to seeing her each week until their relationship changed after the dinner at Reed and Avery's house. He'd replayed the night over in his head, but no matter how hard he tried, he couldn't figure out what could've spooked her.

Part of him wanted to know what happened, what caused her to shut down on him. When he'd asked a couple of weeks ago, she'd out-and-out lied and told him nothing was wrong, confusing him even more. Her open and honest nature was one of the things he admired about her. Why would she start pulling punches now? Common sense told him to quit digging, because sometimes it was better not knowing, but he couldn't let go.

Today was even worse. Not only did she seem distant, she appeared as skittish as a new foal. Ryan's session dragged on, but Colt managed to get through it. When they reached the barn, Jess stood waiting. She and Ryan had become almost inseparable, and whenever he had therapy she met him and together they groomed Chance.

When Colt turned to leave, anxious to escape the tension surrounding him and Stacy, she said, "Could we talk for a minute?"

He froze at the sound of her voice. "I take it this means you're talking to me again."

She nodded. "I'm sorry. Our shooting schedule's been grueling lately. I've been tired and haven't been myself."

The silence he could take, but not the lying. He expected better of her. He was done playing games and pussy footing around the situation. "That's crap and we both know it. What's really going on? Do I have BO or bad breath?"

She smiled at his teasing. She had the best smile.

"Can we just forget it and go back to being friends?"

Having her in his life as a friend was better than this damned polite-acquaintances crap. If that was true, then how come his stomach fell when she'd said the words? "I didn't know we'd stopped being friends."

"Good. I'm glad that's settled." Stacy shifted her stance and her head bobbed up and down like a bobble-head doll. What was going on? "I was also wondering if your offer to go riding was still open."

Something was up. It didn't take a rocket scientist to know that. This time he had to know. "What changed your mind?"

Guilt flashed in her expressive eyes. "I need your help."

His heart sank like a rock tossed into a pond, sending ripples of disappointment through him. He'd been silly to think Stacy changed her mind because she wanted to be with him. Instead she'd asked to go back to the way things were because she needed something from him, and that hurt like a kick in the teeth from an angry stallion.

That's what had kept him and Lynn together so long. She'd needed him. She'd never been on her own. She went from being her parents' daughter to his wife. He took care of everything. As a baby, when Jess got fussy, he spent hours rocking her because Lynn got impatient and frustrated. When Lynn became unhappy with her job at the real-estate management company when a new manager took over, he took on extra work as a hand at Charlie Logan's ranch so she could quit. Then after she'd left him, she'd wanted to come home because she needed someone to take care of her again.

But Stacy's actions hurt even more because she'd always been so open with him.

"Maggie gave me a script change today. I've got to sit on a horse for a scene. I told her I could do it, but now I'm not so sure, and I certainly don't want the first time I get on a horse to be the day we're filming the scene."

He thought about telling Stacy he couldn't help her. That's what he should do.

He couldn't fret about her. He had his daughter to worry about and a therapy program that could financially fall apart at any time. He needed more responsibility like he needed a hole in his work boots.

"I'd like you to talk to the crew. Tell them how to act around horses and what makes them skittish. I know I'm asking a lot, but

would you select the horse for me to ride?"
Fear darkened her eyes to the color of a cold
mountain spring, but she stubbornly pointed
her delicate chin in the air as if she refused
to let her emotions get the best of her.

All he wanted to do was take her in his
arms and hold her until the fear went away.

"I can pick out your horse. The rest will
take time away from my work here."

"I'll pay you for your time." She inched
closer. Her subtle floral scent swirled around
him bringing with it memories of when he'd
held her. "I know what happened to my dad
was a fluke, just one of those weird times
when everything goes wrong and someone
gets hurt, but I'm so scared. The real reason
I want you to be there when we shoot the
scene is I'd feel so much better if you were
there. I know you won't let anything happen
to me. I don't trust anyone but you to keep
me safe. Please."

Damn. She had to go and say that.

*I don't trust anyone but you to keep me
safe.*

How could he say no to that? Only a complete ass would turn her down knowing what
had happened to her father and how scared
she had to be.

"Okay. When's the shoot?"

She flung herself at him, throwing her arms around him, and hugged him. Her dynamite curves pressed up against him. At that moment, with the happy hormones blasting through his system she could've asked him to lasso the moon for her and damned if he wouldn't have said yes.

"Great. The shoot's on Saturday. Could we get together tomorrow for the riding lesson?"

"Sure. We can start with walking around the corral and then head out on one of the tourist trails."

The little voice inside him called him every kind of fool, and said he'd just made a big mistake, but what the hell? He'd made so many in his life. What did one more matter?

Chapter 11

When Stacy arrived at Colt's ranch the next day, she found him in the corral saddling a horse the color of her favorite Starbucks drink, a caramel macchiato. Another equally large sable-colored animal stood already saddled nearby. The sight of Colt, all Western male goodness, his biceps flexing as he lifted the saddle and placed it on the horse sent her pulse as high as the elevation.

You promised Jess there wouldn't be anything between you and Colt but friendship.

That didn't mean she couldn't appreciate his obvious assets, and the man possessed those in spades.

He was so a part of the land around him, so

real, so solid, and not just in a physical sense. When was the last time she'd had someone in her life she could count on? Someone she could call on in the middle of the night, who'd actually answer the phone?

Not since her father died.

She had friends, most of them actresses in the business, but she doubted any of them would be there for her, and the men in her life had come and gone. They got tired of playing second to her career, and her mother and brother for her attention and time.

Colt hadn't been so easy to drive away. Though Lord knows she'd tried. She glanced at the gray clouds as she walked to the corral. "The weather forecast said there's a chance of rain today."

"It's supposed to hold off until tonight."

"That's not what the weatherman on channel eight said."

"You're just using that as an excuse not to go riding."

Of course she was. She'd told Maggie she'd try because she wanted to do what was best for the movie, and while she acted confident when she'd asked Colt for his help the other day, the closer she came to getting up on a horse, the better the idea of letting a stunt woman handle the situation sounded.

"Are you chickening out?"

His taunt stung. She'd never been one to shy away from a challenge or let someone down, and that's what she'd do to Maggie if she backed out now. She'd have to find a stunt woman which would delay the movie further when filming was already behind schedule. That cost the production company money.

"I don't want to get rained on, that's all."

He chuckled. The deep rich sound tickled her senses. The man had the infuriating habit of calling bull whenever she tried to slide something past him. "Next thing you'll be telling me is that the grass is orange." He patted the horse on the neck. "Come over and meet Bess."

"That's the horse you expect me to ride? She's huge."

"In this case, size really doesn't matter. She's the sweetest, most even-tempered horse we've got, and she's practically geriatric, but she's still got her looks. Don't you, girl?"

The horse whinnied in response. Stacy smiled. The man had a way about him.

"I hope time is as easy on my looks as it's been to Bess. She's still beautiful." The horse possessed a graceful beauty. Hopefully her heart matched her looks.

Stacy opened the corral gate and forced

herself to step inside. A gust of wind sent a cloud of dust swirling around her.

It's an omen. The universe is trying to tell me something.

"You'll be fine. Tourists do this all the time. Most of them city slickers like you who've never been on a horse."

"Do I look that scared?"

"Like you're about to shoot the rapids in a barrel." He motioned her to come closer. "I'll hold Bess steady. Grab the saddle horn and put your left foot in the stirrup. Then push off with your right foot and pull yourself into the saddle."

"Why do I think that's not going to be as easy as it sounds?"

"Again, tourists manage this all the time. Half of them not in anywhere the shape you are."

He thought she was in shape? He'd noticed? The heat of her blush crept down her neck.

Remember, just friends.

Oh, but being more could be so much fun.

Trying to focus she grabbed the saddle horn, and after a minute of struggling she managed to get her boot in the stirrup. Then she pulled. She went up, and then came right back down. "I knew getting in the saddle wasn't as easy as you made it sound."

"Try again."

She did, with similar results, except for this time when she started to come back down, his hand cupped her butt and propelled her upward. She glanced down at him from her lofty perch. "Cheap way to cop a feel."

This time he blushed. "Was it as good for you as it was for me?"

It sure was.

She loved how he made her laugh. Why did it feel as though she did so little of that when she was home? Then she glanced down at him. She'd sworn he was joking, and yet, she sensed in a way he wasn't.

Because of his eyes. She knew desire when she saw it in a man's gaze, and her body responded. Heat charged through her, awakening places inside her that had been dormant for so long.

Then Bess nudged him and the spell broke.

She glanced at the mountains around her. Such evidence of endurance. A constant presence. So much like the man beside her.

"How's the view from up there?"

Colt's question made her realize where she was. She waited for panic to slam into her, but the emotion never came. "I'm on a horse, and I'm in one piece."

He smiled at her and she swore she now saw pride in his gaze. "You sure are."

"The view from up here's amazing."

"It's pretty fine from where I stand, too."

Men often told her she was beautiful, but there was something different about Colt's compliments. Maybe because his felt more genuine, and he seemed to admire her as a person. For who she was on the inside.

"Why sir, you'll send a girl's head spinning with pretty words like that," she teased, feeling desperate to break the attraction pulling them together.

She'd told Jess there wouldn't be anything but friendship between them. The words had tumbled out of her easy enough. Too bad following through was turning out to be tougher than she expected.

He mounted his horse and turned to her. "I'll lead the way. Bess knows to follow. Tap her flanks with your heels and she'll follow Jax here."

A twinge of fear rippled through her when Bess shifted under her. "Tell me again how tourists do this all the time and how safe this is."

"We haven't lost a city slicker around here in years. You'll be fine." He flashed her a confident you-can-do-this smile. "If you get scared or want to come back, just say so."

Determined not to let fear rule her, she mumbled a quick prayer and nudged Bess forward. For the first fifteen minutes or so of the ride Stacy gripped the reins so tight her fingers went numb, but the farther they rode, the more she relaxed.

As the ranch faded from view, the foliage grew denser and mountains enveloped them. The stillness surrounded her. The last time she'd been in Colorado she'd missed the city. Its entertainment, its hectic pace with nonstop activity, but not this time. Now she found a peace here her soul craved.

She hadn't realized how much caring for Ryan and dealing with Andrea had weighed on her until she'd gotten out from under some of the pressure. While her mother could still call, the distance kept Andrea from being able to expect Stacy to "pop over" as her mother would say, and deal with every imagined tragedy.

And Colt had worked wonders with Ryan. Her brother was happier than she'd ever seen him. He talked about friends and socialized more since they'd arrived in Estes Park than he had in the entire time since his accident.

His grades had improved and he'd started talking about attending college again.

How could she go back to that bleak life? How could she cope with being that strong again and taking care of everything alone?

Soon she'd have to find a way to do just that, but until then she refused to think about what was to come. Instead she'd concentrate on finishing the movie and enjoying her time here. She deserved that.

After an hour or so of riding, they came upon a clearing. Memories stirred within Colt as he stared at the remnants of a fort he and Reed had built as kids. Their hideout. The fortress where they'd gone to escape their father and his tirades.

Here they'd read books, played cards, or just hung out in the quiet. They could forget for a while and be kids.

He stopped and glanced over his shoulder at Stacy. "I'm ready for lunch. How about you?"

"I'm amazed how hungry I am."

After he dismounted, he walked to where Stacy waited, still seated on Bess. "You need help getting down?"

She shook her head. "Let me try. I would like you to hold her steady, though."

As he stood beside her, his hands on Bess, he said, "Do you realize how far you've come?"

She beamed down at him. "I think I can really do that scene now. Thanks to you."

"You did all the hard work."

"I understand now how the horse therapy helps. There's something about riding that is freeing."

"These programs can help so many people. Ones with mental disabilities. People like Ryan with physical injuries. It's also helping vets who suffer from PTSD." Stacy waited while he retrieved the blanket he'd tied behind his saddle. Then he shook out the old wool and placed it on the ground. He told her to get settled while he returned to Jax and grabbed his saddlebags containing their lunch.

"You're making such a difference for so many people."

When he turned the sight of Stacy sitting under a canopy of Aspen trees, her face bright, her eyes sparkling nearly bowled him over. She looked so at ease, so right sitting here on his land. Maybe this hadn't been such a good idea. He'd better find some self-control real quick.

As he sat on the far edge of the blanket and placed the leather bags between them, she said, "Thank you for helping me prepare for the scene."

He unpacked their simple picnic and handed Stacy a sandwich. "It's egg salad. I figured that was safe. I know you don't eat red meat, but I wasn't sure about chicken or turkey."

"Thanks for remembering. For the record, I do eat chicken and turkey." She took a bite. "This is good. What restaurant did you get the food from?"

"Now I'm insulted. I made lunch."

"Wow. A man who can cook and keeps a house clean enough it could pass the white glove test. How is it that some smart woman hasn't snatched you up?"

"Maybe I just haven't found one I wanted to let grab me."

Until you.

Unable to resist, he leaned over and kissed Stacy. Lightly at first, but when she responded, he couldn't help but deepen the contact.

Thunder rumbled in the distance, and Stacy practically jumped away from him. "We shouldn't have done that."

"If you're waiting for an apology, you're not going to get one."

More thunder rolled toward them. "Still

sticking with your weather prediction?" Stacy teased, easing the tension inside him, but not the physical ache.

He glanced at the sky. The dark clouds on the horizon would be rolling in soon. "We need to head back." He scooped up the remnants of their lunch, shoved everything in his saddlebags and stood. Briefly he considered holding out his hand to help Stacy up, but changed his mind. The less they touched the better.

Ten minutes later, the sprinkles started. The temperature, which had been warm and pleasant when they headed out on the trail, dropped at least twenty degrees when the front moved in. The wind picked up, now coming in from the north.

"I thought you said the rain was supposed to hold off," Stacy chided.

"Guess it's a good thing I'm not a weatherman. Take the path coming up on your right. It'll get us back to the ranch quicker."

Then the heavens opened up, drenching them. He glanced back at Stacy. Worry lined her forehead. "Bess is used to walking in weather like this. She's sure-footed, so there's nothing to fret over. We'll be back to the ranch in a few minutes."

Stacy patted the horse's neck. "I trust her.

I don't think I'll ever be someone who wants to dash around on a horse hell-for-leather—isn't that the expression?"

He nodded, unable to speak. The rain had soaked through her clothes. Her pale blue T-shirt left almost nothing to the imagination, outlining her lacy bra. The cold had hardened her nipples. His body hardened in response.

"But I could see her and I taking a leisurely afternoon stroll every once and a while."

Sure she was more than easy on the eyes and her body could keep a man busy for months exploring every exciting inch of her, but those things weren't what he found most intoxicating. Her grit. Her tenacity. The way she never let anything get the best of her. He couldn't help but admire her. She'd faced her worst fear. She wasn't some dainty little thing that folded when a strong wind blasted her. Those things drew him like a stallion to his favorite mare.

When they reached the ranch, he dismounted and turned to Stacy. As he helped her off her horse, he said, "You know where my room is. Go inside, dry off and get warmed up. I'll see to the horses."

"No, you're cold and wet, too. I can help. Just tell me what to do."

They led the horses into the barn and down

the first row of stalls. "Bess's is the third one down."

While she took Bess, he put Jax in his stall and removed his saddle and bridle. After he set the items in the aisle, he joined Stacy to help with the other horse. "Do you remember where the tack room is?"

"Is that the room where you keep all the horse gear? Where it's all neatly arranged by the horse's name?" He nodded, and Stacy continued. "Has anyone ever mentioned you take organization to a whole new level?"

"You wouldn't say that if you had to spend ten minutes finding the right bridle." He handed her the bridle and told her Jax's was outside his stall. "While you put those away, I'll see to the saddles." *And work on getting my hormones back under control before I dry my clothes from the inside out.*

Five minutes later they sloshed into his house. By the time they reached Colt's room, Stacy knew what it felt like to be a Popsicle. She'd never been so cold in her entire life. She wrapped her arms around her middle, not only for warmth but because her shirt had become completely see-through. At least she'd put on her best ice-blue Victoria's Secret bra today. She'd be even more embarrassed if she was wearing some industrial white thing.

"My bathrobe's still hanging on the bathroom door. When you get that on, toss out your clothes. I'll change out here."

Standing in his bedroom, his presence overwhelmed her. His wet shirt revealed the definition of his rock-hard abs and broad shoulders. His jeans molded to his strong thighs and she refused to think about what else they revealed. So much for being cold. Not a problem now. She practically ran into the bathroom, slamming the door behind her, wincing at the harsh sound.

As she peeled off her soggy clothes her imagination went crazy. All she could think about was Colt a few feet away shedding his clothes, revealing those amazing abs and everything else. Her jeans hit the floor with a thwack and she reached for his robe. She'd thought the last time she slipped into this garment it was intimate. Today was past intimate.

She'd tried so hard to stay away from Colt. To keep from feeling anything for him, but how could she when he'd done so much for Ryan since they'd arrived? He'd given her brother that steady male presence he craved. Ryan had changed so much since they arrived. Not only had he improved physically, going from needing a walker to occasionally only needing a cane, but he'd grown in confidence.

But Colt had helped her in so many ways, too. She enjoyed his company and how he made her laugh. He kept her from taking life too seriously, from becoming overwhelmed. She didn't feel as if she had to always be strong when she was with him, and now, after she'd basically ignored him for weeks, he helped her overcome her fear of horses.

Over a few short weeks, he'd become a part of her life, and she feared she was falling in love with him.

No.

She couldn't. Loving someone started out all sunshine and butterflies, but her relationships never lasted. Loving led to being vulnerable, to disappointment, to unfulfilled expectations and responsibilities.

A knock on the bathroom door broke through her thoughts. "You got those wet clothes off yet?"

After mumbling something like an apology for taking so long, she scooped up her clothes, opened the door and tossed them out. While he went to throw their clothes in the dryer, she located a hair dryer. When she finished with that task, she sat on the toilet. What else could she do to avoid facing Colt? The two of them together with her dressed in his robe? Not a good idea.

A knock sounded on the door again. "You okay in there?"

Startled, she slid off the toilet and landed on the floor with a thud and a squeal, banging her hip in the process.

The door burst open and Colt filled the space. "What happened? Are you all right?"

"Just call me Grace."

He rushed forward to assist her, but she held up a hand to stop him. Once on her feet she took a couple of steps, but his robe tangled around her legs. She reached to free the material, lost her balance and she tumbled smack into Colt. His arms wrapped around her, steadying her.

Desire coursed through her. Lightning crackled closer outside as the storm moved in, mirroring the one brewing inside her.

Her hands cupped his cheeks, his rough stubble scratching her palms as she pulled his face down to hers. Her lips covered his, searching, asking, pleading.

She wanted to feel. She wanted to care. She wanted this man.

More than she'd ever wanted anything in her life. For however long she could have him, even if it was only for the afternoon.

Colt deepened the kiss. As he pressed against her she felt the evidence of his desire. Her hands fumbled with the buttons of his shirt, needing to explore more of him. "I can't do this."

He pulled away, confusion and disappointment flaring in his gaze. "I understand."

"No. It's not what you're thinking. I want you. I can't get these damned buttons undone."

His beaming masculine smile sent a new rush of passion coursing through her. "Let me see what I can do."

Unlike her, he made quick work of the task. Then she slid his shirt off. Her hands caressed his firm flesh. Who needed a gym if hard work could do this for a man's body? Her lips found his again.

His callused hand slipped inside the robe, kneading her breast, sending fire racing through her. She moaned. The hoarse sound filled with need and longing startled her as the soft fabric slid down her body. Lightning cracked outside and thunder rumbled toward them. "A storm's rolled in."

"And not just outside. You're cold." He scooped her into his arms and carried her to the bed. "Scoot under the covers."

She slid between the sheets and then

glanced at him towering beside her. Scars dotted his magnificent chest, but only added to his appeal. Testaments to his courage.

"Undress for me. I want to see you."

"You're so bossy."

"I'm sorry," she stammered, and clutched the blanket up around her chin.

"Nothing to apologize for. No one pushes you around. I like knowing exactly what you want. I don't have to guess what you're thinking."

"Then strip."

"Yes, ma'am."

His fingers shook as he unbuckled his belt, and slowly lowered his zipper. His gaze locked on hers as he slid his jeans past his hips, revealing himself to her. The sight of him, strong, proud and pulsing with desire for her, fueled her need. An image of him like this, except wearing his cowboy hat, flashed in her mind. He looked so damned sexy in that hat. She'd have to ask him to pose like that for her. More thunder rattled around them. Or was that her heart?

Colt thought he'd come right then and there when Stacy told him to strip. As he kicked off his jeans, she licked her lips, and he closed his eyes, trying to harness his control before he embarrassed himself. Warms hands clasped his heated flesh as her lips moved over his chest.

For a moment he lost himself to his emotions, his desire. The fever built inside him, threatening to burn him to cinders. He needed her in his arms. He yanked back the blankets and practically pounced on her.

It had been so long, and making love had never been like this. Frenzied. Consuming. Real. He had to slow down, but he couldn't.

He suckled her breast while his hands found her heated core. Her moans echoed through him, fueling his ardor, driving him to heights he never knew existed. As he caressed her, her hands clutched his shoulders. Her teeth nipped at his neck.

"You're so beautiful, and not just on the outside." He kissed her, his tongue mating with hers.

He felt the waves rock through her as she reached her peak. Her nails dug into his shoulders. "Now. I want you inside me now."

He stilled. Birth control. He didn't have anything. "I didn't plan for this. It's been so long." He swallowed hard and told himself not to babble. "I don't have a condom."

"It's your lucky day." She kissed him lightly and smiled. The smile of a satisfied woman.

Then she crawled out of bed. As he stared at her beautiful body displayed for him, he couldn't follow her train of thought.

That's because there isn't a drop of blood left going to your brain.

She found her purse on a chair, dug around inside and retrieved a foil packet. "I have one."

A man had to love a woman who was prepared.

The thought ricocheted through him. Did he love Stacy? He admired her. Lusted after her big-time. Appreciated her spunk, but love?

Then her frenzied hands were on him again, and he forgot everything but her. His hands teased her sensitive flesh, needing to ignite her passion, but she shoved him down on the bed and straddled him.

As she situated herself on his heated flesh, he reveled in the pleasure coursing through him. They moved together. He stared up into her gorgeous face, reveling in the passion returning to expressive eyes. Passion for him. Clear and mesmerizing. His gaze locked with hers as he caressed her, bringing her to another peak. Only then did he let go. Wave after wave crashed over him, breaking him and somehow putting him back together.

What had he done?

He'd connected with a woman on a level he never knew possible. Had he also made the biggest mistake of his life?

Don't go there. Savor this. Don't think beyond now.

While the storm inside them had subsided, the one outside hadn't. Lightning continued to slash across the sky and thunder rumbled around them.

He felt more content than he had in years. Being with Stacy felt right. The question was, where did they go from here? He cared for her, but he refused to examine his nagging thoughts about love. Right now his life couldn't take any more upheaval. Jess and his therapy program had to be his top concerns. The most he could offer Stacy was a casual relationship, but would that offend her? Make her think she was good enough to sleep with, but not worth any type of commitment?

Casual relationship. The phrase rubbed him the wrong way. He wasn't the love-'em-and-leave-'em type, and that's exactly what it felt like he was doing.

Thunder rumbled outside. He lay there fulfilled and content, Stacy's gentle curves nestled against him, heating him up all over again, and knew they should talk about what happened between them. Hell, they should've talked about where things were headed before they tumbled into bed, but he figured better late than never.

"I guess we just became more than friends," he joked, not knowing how else to bring up the subject.

"You heard that comment?"

"That and a little more. Thanks for what you said to Jess. I had no idea she was carrying around so much guilt over her mom. She and I had a great talk about everything after that. She really opened up to me, and we cleared the air about some things."

"She loves you so much."

He shook his head. "I still can't believe she asked you what your intentions were. I said while I appreciated the concern, that's not her job. I'm an adult and can take care of myself."

He failed to mention how damned embarrassing her conversation had been. No man should have to discuss his love life, or lack thereof, with his teenage daughter.

"I don't want you getting the wrong impression about what happened between us," Stacy said as she slid away from him. "I don't want you thinking I'm expecting anything from you. I'm usually not so impulsive. Not that I didn't enjoy what happened, I did. It was amazing, but there can't be anything other than something casual between us. Our lives are so different. We don't even live in the same state."

He noticed whenever she was nervous she talked a mile a minute. Good to know he wasn't the only one feeling uneasy.

"I wasn't about to get down on one knee, if that's what you were thinking." His words came out with a bite rather than as a light-hearted joke as he intended. Hadn't she said exactly what he'd been thinking? So why was his pride bruised? "We're both adults. We enjoy each other's company. There's nothing wrong with that."

"Except we're both responsible for a teenager."

What kind of example are we setting? The words hung unspoken between them, and where did they go from here?

Sleeping with each other once? They might be able to keep that from Jess and Ryan. Carrying off an affair? No way.

What were they going to do?

Lightning cracked close, too close, and before the light faded the deafening roar of thunder shook the walls. Colt jumped out of bed. "Damn. That hit something."

"Are you sure?"

He didn't answer, but scooped up his jeans off the floor where he'd dropped them beside the bed earlier. He shrugged them on and moved to the window. "The barn's on fire! I've got to get the horses out."

Then he bolted out the door.

Stacy leaped out of bed, her heart and mind racing. She dug through her purse again and located her phone. As she dashed through the house to retrieve her clothes from the dryer, she called 911. She explained the situation to the dispatcher and asked the woman to send the fire department. That done, Stacy dressed and ran outside after Colt.

The driving rain pelted her skin soaking her again as she raced for the barn. Flames licked at the back side of the structure's roof. At least it was the area farthest away from the horses. The barn door stood open. She darted inside. Horses' panicked shrieks filled the air. Smoke stung her nose and lungs. The gray haze burned her eyes.

As she ran toward the stalls, she scanned the area for Colt, finding him down the first row. "What can I do?"

"Get out. It's not safe in here."

"I'm not leaving you alone to deal with this. I won't let these animals die." *Or you.*

Something could fall on him. The smoke could get to him and no one would ever know. She refused to think about what else could happen.

Colt yanked open a stall door and Babe charged out. "Go away, Stacy. Call 911."

"I already did." She grabbed his arm. "We don't have time to argue. Tell me what to do, damn it."

"Open stall doors. The horses should get out on their own. If one won't I'll take care of it."

She nodded. "I'll get the other row."

He grabbed her hand. "You sure?"

She nodded and squeezed his hand before she ran off toward the other stalls. Wood being consumed crackled around them. Sweat poured down her face, blurring her vision as the heat increased. She pulled open a stall door, jumped back, watched the horse race out and moved on. Her breathing grew labored as she moved down the row.

When the last horse was free, Stacy ran back to where she'd left Colt. "Colt, are you done? Where are you?"

A horse's shrill screech of a panic cut through the fire's roar. "Go. I'll follow in a minute."

She hesitated at the far end of the row. No,

she wouldn't leave until he went with her. As she ran down the aisle toward him she saw him struggling with a huge black horse. The animal pulled the rope from Colt's grasp and reared.

"Colt!"

Stacy's screams reverberated around her. All she could see was her father being crushed under a similar massive animal's hooves.

History was repeating itself.

Chapter 12

No. Stacy refused to let this happen again. She'd been too young to prevent her father from dying, but she *would* save Colt.

The horse's hooves pounded his chest, knocking him to his knees. His arms covered his head as he fought to stand. The animal reared again.

"No!" Stacy screamed as she waved her arms and ran. "Colt, tell me what to do."

In the few seconds it took her to reach him, he'd managed to stand and was pulling his bandana out of his back pocket. Then he grabbed the horse's lead rope and handed it to her. "Talk to him and hold on. If I can get his eyes covered, he should calm down."

"Hey, big boy. It's okay. I know you're scared. My dad used to sing to me when I was afraid." The words to *Put On a Happy Face* from one of her father's favorite musical, *Bye Bye Birdie,* flowed out of her, calming both her and the horse. The animal stopped pulling against her. His movements grew less frantic, until he calmed enough for Colt to tie the bandana around his eyes.

Then Colt took the rope from her. "Let's get the hell out of here."

Sirens screamed in the distance as Colt, with Stacy beside him, led the horse out of the barn to discover the storm had moved on. Rain sprinkled his skin as he opened the corral for the animal to join the other horses nervously milling around. Then everything hit him at once. How reckless she'd been. How he could've lost her, and how without her he'd more than likely be dead right now. He reached out and his soot-covered hands cupped her face as he kissed her lightly. Then he leaned his forehead against hers.

"Thank you for not following directions. If you'd listened to me and left when I told you to, I'd be dead."

He kissed her again and then interlocked his hand with hers to still their shaking. Fate could be brutally fickle and had a way of making a man see what really mattered in life.

"I wasn't going to let what happened to my dad happen to you."

She hadn't left him. She'd fought with him. The city woman, hotshot actress who when she'd arrived had been afraid to be near a horse, had battled a fire and her fear to not only to help save every animal, but him, as well.

"Are you okay? The horse kicked you in the chest."

"I'll be bruised and sore tomorrow, but I suspect the whole thing looked worse to you than it actually was." He looked toward the barn, as the firefighters worked to control the flames still licking at the barn. "I'd never have gotten all the horses out in time if you hadn't helped. You have got to be the strongest woman I've ever met. Damn woman, you're amazing."

"Tell me you have insurance," Stacy said as she, too, stared at the scorched barn, the firefighters having gotten the blaze under control.

"I do, but I've got a huge deductible. That was one of the ways I cut operating costs so I could get the program up and running sooner." He rubbed his forehead as his mind raced to list the things he'd need to do over the next few days. Call his insurance agent. Double-check his list of the barn's contents. Find someone to stable his horses until the barn was inhabitable again.

"I bet the community and anyone who's gone through your program will help you come up with the deductible. We can have a fund-raiser to raise the cash and replace anything insurance won't cover. Bring a bridle and help Healing Horses rebuild."

We. He liked the sound of that.

"That's a great idea."

"I'll work on jotting down some ideas. I can talk to Nannette to see what she thinks."

Had Lynn ever been this much a partner in his life and what mattered to him? He mentally shook himself. He had to stop thinking about his wife. She was dead and gone. That marriage was in the past. He'd told Stacy not to let what happened with her father affect her now. He needed to do the same. He had to let go of Lynn, of his anger and his disappointment. No more. He was done viewing the world though the haze of his failed marriage. He was finished keeping everyone at arm's length.

Starting with Stacy. What a woman. She

made him feel like he wasn't alone, looked like a first-class diamond and was just as tough.

He wouldn't find a better woman if he searched for the rest of his life. His heart expanded. He'd fallen in love with Stacy. No doubt about it. As he listened to her spin ideas for the fund-raising event, he didn't know where his relationship with her would go, but he'd hold on to her for as long as she was here and enjoy the ride.

The next morning when Colt arrived at the Twin Creeks movie set along with Jess and Ryan, Stacy met them near the barn. Seeing her dressed in Wranglers that showed off her great curves, cowboy boots, her blond hair pulled back in a ponytail, a cowboy hat perched on her head sent a jolt through him. At first, he almost didn't recognize her, but damn she looked fine. Almost as good as she had in his bed yesterday afternoon.

All he wanted to do was put his arms around her and tell her how lonely his bed had been last night without her there with him.

How did other people juggle having a love life and being a single parent? Someone ought to write a manual. After Stacy greeted Jess and her brother, she glanced at him, mumbled a greeting and blushed the prettiest shade of pink. At least he wasn't the only one who wasn't sure how to handle things this morning.

"You two are going to be bored," Stacy said to Ryan and Jess. "Making movies isn't as glamorous as everything thinks. It's a lot of doing the same scene over and over again."

"Maggie said she could use us as extras in the scene that you're filming after you finish this one," Jess said, her young face beaming with excitement.

"Do you know where Maggie is?" Ryan asked. "She said to check in with her when we got here and she'd tell us what we're going to be doing."

Stacy pointed toward the trailer off to her right. "She should be in there double-checking things for the shoot."

Once the kids left, Colt considered bringing up what happened between them yesterday, but what could he say? That he was confused as hell about their relationship, had no idea how to handle things between them now and did she have any suggestions?

When the awkward silence stretched as he stood there like a scared school boy, Stacy finally said, "You don't have to be here. I'm sure with the fire yesterday you have important things to take care of. Since Maggie agreed to let me ride Bess, I'll be all right."

The day before friends and neighbors started arriving with horse trailers to move his animals even before the firefighters put out the fire. "The most important things are done. We got the horses moved yesterday, and I already talked to the insurance agent this morning. He'll be out this afternoon to look at the damage and start working on the claim. Until he does that, there's not much I can do."

"If you're sure."

Her words said one thing, but the uncertainty in her gaze told him something else. He brushed his knuckles across her cheek. "I promised I'd be here for you, and I'm a man of my word."

"That's what I was hoping you'd say. I know everything will be okay, but I'm still edgy. Having you here makes me feel so much better. Safer."

This woman had invaded his life, every nook and cranny. Quickly, thoroughly and with surprising force. The thought rippled through him leaving him stunned.

The catch was she wouldn't stick around. Ryan's ten-week therapy had only a couple of sessions left. The movie was set to finish shooting a week after that.

Their days were numbered.

Before he figured out how to respond, Maggie called for everyone's attention. "We're set to start." She motioned for Colt to come forward. "Everyone here knows what happened to Stacy's father. Because of that, we're taking extra precautions. She and I thought it would be a good idea if we went over a few horse basics before we started shooting."

Colt spent the next few minutes going over the fundamentals with the crew. No loud noises. No sudden unexpected moves. If the horse started pawing the ground or seemed at all nervous, he'd let Maggie know, and they'd stop filming until he figured out what the issue was. Maggie said Colt didn't need to consult with her. If he felt they needed to take a break, he was to call cut. His job was to remain focused on Stacy and ensure her safety.

After talking to the crew, he led Bess to the pasture fence and helped Stacy mount. "I'm so glad Maggie was okay with me riding my BFF here." Stacy leaned down and patted the horse's neck. "Good thing you still have your looks, girlfriend. Most actresses your age aren't so lucky."

"You two are quite a pair."

She flashed him a weak smile.

The woman and the horse had a lot in common. Both beautiful, sturdy stock, dependable and made of steel, but with a heart of pure marshmallow—all sweet and soft.

"You'll be fine, but I'm right over there if you need me. You ready?"

She nodded, and he placed his hands over her as they clutched the reins so tight her knuckles whitened. Her grip relaxed under his. "All set."

He squeezed her hand one more time. "Thata girl."

Then Colt joined Maggie and the camera crew. That way he'd remain close to Stacy and the action, but wouldn't risk getting in the shots.

Maggie called for action. Stacy nudged Bess with her heels and the pair started walking along the fence. The actor in the scene rode in from the west on a three-wheeler, stopping a few feet away, jumped off the vehicle and made his way to Stacy where he helped her dismount. Then they talked while they walked toward the barn with Stacy leading Bess.

Simple.

Stacy relaxed once Maggie called cut. While her performance had been mediocre at best, she was thrilled she made it through the first take with nothing going wrong. When Maggie approached, Stacy said, "That was awful, but now I've got my nerves under control, I'll do better on the next take."

"It's okay. I expected you to be little uptight to start. We're not going to rush this." Maggie wrapped her arm around Stacy's shoulders. "Are you doing all right? We can take a break if you need to."

"I'm fine. Let's give it another try."

A few takes later Maggie claimed she had what she was looking for, but she wanted to try a different spin on the scene before she called it good. She wanted one more take with Brandon upping the emotion a little and showing more anger. Stacy sat on Bess watching the actor approach in the three-wheeler. As he came closer she waited for him to slow down. He didn't. If anything he accelerated. Her stomach tightened. Bess shifted nervously under her, as if the animal also sensed something was wrong.

"Get out of the way!" Brandon shouted. "The accelerator's stuck."

Stacy tugged on Bess's reins, trying to turn the horse away from the fence. They had to get out of the way. Voices screaming orders created an indiscernible chaos pounding in her head. She couldn't think. Couldn't remember anything Colt told her about controlling a horse.

"Toss me the reins and grab the saddle horn."
Colt.

The death grip on her heart loosened as she followed his instructions. He grabbed the reins and led her and Bess away.

Brandon jumped off the three-wheeler, but the vehicle barreled forward, crashing into the fence near where she and Bess had been. The sound of metal colliding with wood and concerned voices echoed in Stacy's ears.

She glanced at Colt, and started shaking. The situation could have gone so differently if he hadn't been there. Bless that take-charge attitude of his. He'd known she needed help before she could even call out to him.

His hands slipped around her waist, strong and warm, comforting her as he helped her off Bess. "I didn't know what to do. I couldn't remember anything you told me about how to tell a horse where to go."

She leaned into him, her head resting on his strong chest. The hammering of his heart pounded against her cheek. "You're safe now."

"Thanks to you."

The crew rushed forward to help Brandon, who was unhurt except for a few scrapes to his arms. Slowly the noises quieted, and then Stacy heard Ryan's screams.

Brandon's mishap triggered Ryan's memories of his accident. Her gaze searched for Ryan, finding him huddled against the barn. When Jess approached him, he shoved away from his friend almost knocking her down. Stacy raced toward him, but the closer she got, the more he looked as if he would bolt. "Ryan, it's me, Stacy."

She wrapped her arms around him, trying to comfort him and still his shaking, but he broke free. His eyes glazed over, he looked like a cornered animal. She moved toward him, but he backed away.

"Watch out!"

"Ryan, look at me," Stacy begged.

She thought he'd gotten past this. His nightmares had subsided. He'd been so happy lately, almost back to his old self, but here they were with him lost inside his head, reliving the tormenting images of his accident.

Stacy glanced over her shoulder to find Colt. Her gaze locked with his, pleading with him to help her. "He won't let me touch him. What can I do?"

"Nothing." Colt inched forward. "Hey, buddy. I'm here." He moved forward another step. "Talk to me, Ryan."

"No! Get out of the way!"

The vacant look in his gaze told Stacy

he wasn't really seeing anyone or anything around him, only the past.

"Ryan, look at me. Talk to me. It's Colt."

Colt continued to inch closer until he stood in front of Ryan. The pain and guilt etched on her brother's face broke her heart. "Officer, I didn't see him. I swear."

Touching Ryan's shoulder, Colt said, "It's okay, Ryan."

Colt encircled her brother in his strong embrace. Ryan shoved against him, but couldn't break free. "It was so awful. He came out of nowhere. I didn't mean to hit him."

"I know."

"It was so awful. He almost died." Sobs erupted from Ryan. His head rested on Colt's broad chest. "I heard from him the other day. He'll never walk again. I'm getting better. I might even walk on my own again. I don't have any right to be doing this well while he's in a wheelchair for the rest of his life."

"I get it. I feel the same way a lot of days. Some of my buddies didn't come home. Some lost arms or legs, but not me. I came home in one piece. Why did I when they didn't?"

"How do you live with it?"

She hadn't realized Ryan kept in contact with the man he hit, or that he carried enough blame for a lifetime. No matter how much she sympathized or wanted to understand, she couldn't comprehend how he felt over what happened. But Colt understood because a similar survivor's guilt gnawed at him.

"I try to live my life in a way that honors them. I try to make a difference."

Stacy stared at the two men in front of her as emotions crashed over her, almost bringing her to her knees with their force.

Two men capable of such incredible compassion yet forged of iron.

And she loved both of them more than she dreamed possible.

Her knees threatened to buckle under her as the realization slammed into her. How had she let this happen? Andrea fell in love every five minutes, but Stacy knew better than to give her heart away.

Over the years she'd wondered if she ever loved any of her boyfriends. Now she knew that she hadn't.

A cowboy who lived in Colorado? Why did it have to be a man like that when she finally fell in love? She thought her mother picked the wrong men? Like mother, like daughter.

Maggie joined her. "Colt's amazing. He seems good with Ryan."

Too bad he was so wrong for her in so many ways because Maggie was right. "He understands Ryan and what he's going through in a way I never could."

"After this afternoon's events, I've decided to use the last take of the scene with you and Brandon. We'll call it a day and pick up tomorrow."

"You had a full day scheduled. Stopping now will cost you a lot of money." Stacy glanced at Ryan. He appeared much calmer. His fidgeting had ceased, and his face looked more relaxed as he and Colt stood near the barn talking. That's what Ryan needed right now—time with a man who understood what he was going through. She told Maggie to hold off on letting everyone go until she talked to Colt and Ryan.

"How about you two get out of here?" Stacy said when she joined them by the barn.

"You need Colt here for the scene," Ryan said, his eyes clearer than when she'd spoken with him before.

"We're calling that scene good, so I'll be fine. Get out of here. Do some guy stuff."

As she stared at Colt, she prayed he received her silent message. *Get Ryan out of here. Talk to him. Help him cope with what he's feeling.*

He caught her gaze over her brother's shoulder, and nodded in understanding. How could he know her better in such a short time than friends she'd known for years?

"Ryan, I could use your help sorting through the equipment in the barn to see what's salvageable and what needs to be replaced."

"That sounds a lot better than being an extra in the movie. I only agreed to it because Jess asked me to."

They talked to Jess and decided since she still wanted to be in the movie that Stacy would bring her home later. Once the guys left, the rest of the Stacy's day proved uneventful. They filmed another scene around the ranch, a get-together with the area ranchers with Jess as an extra. With that done, Maggie wrapped up early for the day.

When Stacy dropped Jess off, she found Colt in the rocking chair on the porch. "What're you doing out here?"

"Enjoying the quiet and the sunset." He stood. "Ryan is playing video games and the noise was getting to me."

She glanced over her shoulder and gasped at the beauty before her. The setting sun was just dipping behind the mountains, darkening them. A fiery glow spread across the sky. "It's beautiful. I could sit here for hours."

"I do some of my best thinking in this chair."

"I can see why. Something about being here has cleared my head in a lot of ways." Since coming here she'd taken a long, hard look at her life and found it lacking, except for her relationship with her brother. The thought reminded her of why she'd come. "Thanks for all you did for Ryan today. How's he doing?"

As she followed Colt inside he asked her to stay for dinner and then said, "He's doing better. We took inventory here to see what we could salvage. After that we went to Twin Creeks to check on the horses. There's something about working with a horse that calms a person. That kid's been holding a lot in. He knows how much your mother dumps on you and he doesn't want to do the same thing."

Once in the kitchen she sat at the table and tried to process what he'd said. "I had no idea he was thinking that."

This was the kind of kitchen she'd dreamed of having, cozy and warm. The kind of room a family congregated in at the end of the day to reconnect and share their lives. Truly share. Where everyone listened because they cared about each other.

"We spent a lot of time talking about the accident. He's beating himself up for not anticipating someone could walk out from between the parked cars. He thinks if he'd been a better driver, he could've avoided hitting the man. He keeps replaying the scene in his mind trying to figure out what he could've done differently."

"He's being too hard on himself. The police investigated and saw no reason to charge him. They determined he'd done nothing wrong."

"He knows that, but it doesn't make him feel any less guilty because he's walking and the guy he hit isn't."

"Like you feel guilty because you came home and friends you served with didn't?" He nodded, and pain flickered in his gaze. "How do I help him deal with what he's feeling?"

"You can't. He's got to come to terms with it."

"Have you?"

"Some days, I think so. Then others I'm sure I haven't even started. That's how it'll be for Ryan. It would help if he didn't spend so much time alone. That gives him too much time to think. He says you've been putting in long hours on the set."

"I can't help it. Filming is behind and Maggie's worried about money. She says we've got to wrap up on time."

"Don't get your dander up. I wasn't criticizing, merely stating facts, and I've got a solution. He can come here after school."

"This isn't your problem. I'll figure something out. I could ask Maggie if Ryan could come to the set after school."

"Why do that when I've offered a better solution? Let me help."

His words, said with a good amount of irritation in his voice, made her think. Why hadn't she just been thankful for his offer instead of insisting she could take care of everything on her own?

In her experience whenever anyone offered help there were strings attached. They wanted something from her. Either that or they failed to follow through. Look at Andrea. How many times had she promised to be there for her children only to have "something come up?"

But Colt was different. "I guess I'm a little out of practice accepting help. Thank you."

How could she ever repay him for everything he'd done for her? Worse yet, how would she ever be able to walk away from him?

A few days later as Colt stood inside the front door of Halligan's with Stacy beside him, greeting people as they arrived for the fund-raiser to help Healing Horses cover the insurance deductible, he marveled at the changes in his life. Ryan and Jess had settled into a routine. Their friendship seemed to be a stabilizing force in both their lives. After he picked them up from school, they sat in the kitchen doing homework. Then they either worked with the horses or played video games until dinner. If Stacy finished shooting in time, she joined them and the four of them sat together, ate and discussed the day's events.

Like countless other families.

After dinner he and Stacy either snuggled on the couch to watch TV or sat on the porch in their rocking chairs. He smiled thinking of how Stacy had hugged him when she showed up to find the chair he'd bought her next to his on the porch.

He was happier than he'd been in years. Stacy had slipped into his life and turned it upside down, but in a good way. He enjoyed being with her, even though he spent the majority of his time trying to figure out a way to get her alone. Not that it had gotten him anything other than a few minutes here and there to share a few kisses and some heated necking.

Lord help him. How was he ever going to let her walk out of his life?

She'd helped him in so many ways. This

fund-raiser was another perfect example. Without him even asking, Stacy organized the event with Nannette's help. The pair met with Nannette's daughter-in-law Elizabeth, a former New York City advertising executive who now ran a local ad agency, to design posters and put them up around town. Then Stacy talked to Avery's friend Emma and asked Maroon Peak Pass to play for the event.

"Thanks for doing all this. I'm surprised Mick agreed to let me in the place. He's still mad at me for the fight with Carpenter."

"You'll have to thank Nannette for that. She's the one who sweet-talked him and promised there wouldn't be any trouble. She even talked to Travis and told him if he came within fifty feet of Halligan's tonight, he'd answer to her."

Colt laughed. "That would put the fear of God into any man. Even Carpenter isn't foolish enough to cross Nannette."

"No kidding. I think we should send her to Washington. She'd have the nation's problems fixed in a week."

"Now that would shake things up."

He shifted his stance, their conversation oddly trivial and awkward after everything they'd been through.

"Great idea, having this fund-raiser," Brian, an old friend of Reed's and one of the city's Board of Trustees, said when he walked through the front door. "What you do for the disabled in the area is so important to the community."

Colt introduced Stacy. "This was her idea. She did all the work. I just showed up."

"I heard you helped Colt get the horses out when the barn caught fire."

"I did what anyone would have done," Stacy replied.

Not every woman would've charged in. Would Lynn have risked her life to save his? More than likely she'd have called 911, and told him to forget about the horses and save himself.

Not Stacy. She dived in and helped. She stood by his side.

"She did more than that." Colt explained how the horse had kicked him and Stacy had calmed the animal enough for him to cover its eyes and lead him out. "Without her, I might have died in that fire."

"Who would've thought a fancy city-girl actress like you had that much gumption in her?" Brian's voice pulled Colt away from his thoughts.

"I'll take that as a compliment," Stacy said with a huge grin on her face.

"Why wouldn't you since that's what it was?" Brian glanced at her, confusion clouding his plain features. "You're all right."

"She certainly is," Colt said.

And he'd fallen for her. He hadn't even known Cupid was in town, much less seen the arrow heading his way.

Chapter 13

Brian's simple statement and the admiration shining in Colt's gaze set off a ripple of pride in Stacy. Tonight was different than the last time she'd been in Halligan's. No whispers and pointed glances shot her way. No questions about her time on *Finding Mrs. Right* and how she felt being tossed over on national TV. Instead she'd received compliments for her quick thinking and bravery. She felt as if she belonged.

Even when Griffin and Maggie walked in that feeling didn't change. How could she be uncomfortable around them when her heart had never been involved? Her pride? Sure, but never her heart. When he'd proposed to

Maggie at the finale she'd been more worried about her career and upset over looking like a fool. Never once during their dates did her heart flutter when Griffin looked at her. He never made her want more out of life. Like Colt did.

"Thanks for coming out tonight to support Healing Horses," Colt said.

"We're family. Where else would we be?" Griffin replied and slapped his friend on the back.

They have no idea how lucky they are. What a gift having a family like theirs is.

Maggie turned to her. "How's your brother doing? I feel so awful about what happened."

"I think him melting down was a blessing in disguise. I didn't know that Ryan had been in contact with the man from the accident. Now that's out in the open, and we can deal with what he's feeling. He had a session with a psychologist and that's helped, too."

"Two more days of shooting. Can you believe it?"

She flinched at Maggie's statement. Not tonight. She didn't want to think about leaving.

"I didn't know you were that close to being done with the movie." Beside her she swore Colt stiffened.

"All we've got is one more scene to film,

and based on how great yesterday's rushes were, we should breeze right through that," Maggie continued.

Colt's hawklike gaze zeroed in on Stacy and she resisted the urge to squirm. "Do you know when you're leaving?"

Ask me to stay. Tell me you can't bear the thought of me leaving you.

"Originally Ryan and I thought we'd fly back next week, but I don't have to be back in L.A. until I start shooting my next movie in six weeks."

"You could stick around for a while."

Colt's comment wasn't exactly what she hoped to hear, but it was something. What harm would there be in staying a few weeks longer? She could take some time for herself and unwind. When was the last time she'd done that? Plus, the extra break from Andrea would be another benefit, but more importantly she would have more time with Colt to see what developed between them. "I could use a vacation. I could take time to do all the touristy type things I keep hearing everyone talk about before I head back."

"I bet you could use some time off. That director of yours is a slave driver," Griffin added, only to have his wife swat him on the arm.

"I'd be happy to play tour guide," Colt offered. "We could start with the tour of The Stanley Hotel. They filmed *The Shining* miniseries there."

"Spring break's in a couple of weeks. The transition would be easier for Ryan then. He wouldn't have to miss any school."

That's not why you want to stay, and you know it.

No, but the rationalization sounded like the perfect one for public consumption. That way if things didn't work out with Colt she had a way to salvage her pride.

"Colt, the band would like you to say something before they start playing," Nannette said as she joined them.

While Colt stood on stage, Stacy and Nannette sat at a back table. "Thanks, everyone, for coming tonight to support Healing Horses. That's one thing I've always loved about this community, how everyone pulls together when someone's in need."

"I've got to say, you've surprised me," Nannette said. "The girl that showed up at my ranch never would've taken the time to do what you've done for Colt by organizing this."

"Colt's done so much for Ryan, it's the least I can do."

He's done so much for me.

She heard him talking about his work with Healing Horses and a thought popped into her head. He mends people.

He'd done that with Ryan. He'd mended her as well, and she hadn't even known she needed putting back together. Because of him, she didn't feel alone for the first time since her father died. Colt had taken some of the weight off her shoulders by helping with Ryan. He'd given her a safe place to unwind at the end of the day. A person to confide in, bounce ideas off of, someone to sit and be with if she didn't feel like talking. He'd been the first person in her life in so long who had given more than he'd taken.

She thought of the two of them sitting in rockers on the front porch. A sunset never looked more beautiful than it did from her spot in the comfortable oak rocker he'd bought for her and placed on his front porch beside his. She could see herself sitting there with him in her old age. The realization rippled through her leaving her weak. She bit her lip.

She loved the man with all her heart, but loving someone wasn't always enough to make a relationship work in the real world.

"There's more to what's going on with you

and Colt, and we both know it." The older woman's knowing eyes stared through her.

The words that she and Colt were just friends stuck in her throat. She wouldn't lie to Nannette, and even if she did, the older woman would see it for what her words were—a big, stinky pile of cow manure.

"Movie sets are funny places, almost a world of its own. The cast, crew and the people we come in contact with become a family of sorts. At least during filming." Then shooting wrapped up. People said they'd keep in touch, but Stacy discovered that to be one of those polite phrases individuals spouted with all sincerity but failed to follow through on. Or, they commented on each other's Facebook posts or tweets, and occasionally texted each other, but that wasn't really being involved in someone's life. "Unfortunately, a lot of the relationships forged on the set fade once the movie's done."

What if her relationship with Colt was one that grew out of close proximity and shared emotional events—Ryan's therapy, facing her fear of horses, Colt's barn fire and Jess's revelations about her mother—but it lacked the substance to last?

"Colt cares about you. I see it in his eyes

when he watches you when you're not looking."

But did he care enough to try to make things work between them? Enough to tackle the issues keeping them apart, like the fact that they lived in two different states? "I'm not so sure."

"You'll never know if you don't give it a chance."

"It's not that simple. My life is in California. That's where my mom lives. That's where my career is."

"Sometimes what we think is important is really just noise keeping us from hearing that little voice inside telling us what we really want our life to be about."

Noise? The clatter in her life was deafening. Colt quieted some of the din for her. He had a way of cutting to the heart of the matter.

He'd shown her what life could be like when there was give and take. Like yesterday. Andrea had called during the lunch break. She didn't know what to do. As if she ever did. Things weren't going as well as her mother hoped since Grant moved back. He'd been coming home late, and when Andrea questioned him about his whereabouts, he accused her of not trusting him. Her mother went on to say Grant often wasn't answering his cell when she tried to call him and he seemed distant. Then Andrea tearfully added she couldn't wait for Stacy to come home.

Stacy knew the signs, having seen them time and time again with her mother's other relationships. Andrea latched on to a man, but then became so fearful of losing him she clung to him with a desperation that drove him away.

Not once did her mother ask about how the movie was going. Nor did she ask about Ryan and if the therapy had produced any results. Unlike Colt who always asked about her day and actually cared what she said.

Stacy stared at Nannette. Strong, capable and nurturing. So unlike Andrea. *Too bad we don't get to choose our family.*

"It's not that simple. I have Ryan to think of, and my mother's had a difficult life. Her marriage is on the rocks—"

"Life's hard for everyone."

Stacy froze, afraid she'd offended Nannette. What was she thinking? Nannette was a widow and a cancer survivor. "I'm sorry. That was thoughtless of me to say after everything you've gone through. Unfortunately, my mom doesn't possess your strength. She relies on me so much."

The older woman placed her hand over Stacy's. "You're not your mother's keeper. She's a grown woman. You've got the right to live your own life. That's part of a parent's job—to let go."

That sounded wonderful, but how did she get Andrea to see the fact?

She glanced at Colt on the stage. "I want to thank Maroon Peak Pass for playing tonight. Now I've yammered on too long, so I'll get out of the way for them to take over." Colt turned to Emma and said something before he left the stage.

A minute later when he stood beside Stacy, he nodded toward Nannette and asked the older woman to excuse them. Then he slipped his hand in Stacy's, and her heart tripped. "Dance with me. We didn't get to do that the last time we were here."

"There are things I need to check on—"

"I'm here to see to things. You two go on," Nannette said, a bold matchmaker smile on her face.

"We've had a request for a slow one to start off the night, so grab your honey and come out on the dance floor," Emma announced.

Colt leaned down and whispered in Stacy's ear. "I need you in my arms."

A shudder rippled through her as his heated breath fanned over her skin. How could she resist his husky plea and heated gaze, especially when she wanted him to hold her, too?

As she followed him onto the dance floor she told herself that tonight she'd forget about everything but Colt. When his hands slid around her waist, she leaned into him, savoring the feel of him. His strength seeped into her. If only she could bottle that feeling and take it home with her to use when dealing with Andrea left her weak and feeling drained.

"Not being able to have you in my arms has been killing me."

She'd missed him holding her. They'd seen each other every day since Ryan started going to Colt's house after school. The four of them ate dinner together most nights. If shooting ran late, Colt kept something warm for her and then he kept her company while she ate, but they hadn't been alone.

"Kids, even teenagers, definitely complicate things, don't they?"

"I'm just glad they had plans with friends tonight so we could have some time alone."

Stacy laughed and glanced at the couples around them on the dance floor. "I don't know what your definition of alone is, but this isn't mine."

"We could sneak out."

"Of a fund-raiser for your program? Not likely, or in good taste."

"So when would it be okay for us to cut out? And keep in mind the movie the kids are at ends at ten-forty."

Just the thought of being with him again made her all tingly inside, but making love with him was the last thing she should do when she was leaving soon. What she needed to do was wind things down with him or decide where they went from here.

What if she brought up the idea of them continuing to see each other and he smiled, said no, thanks, but wished her luck? But wasn't that what she wanted when she first became involved with him? No strings attached? She'd wanted things in her life—like a mother who acted like a parent—but fate never cooperated. Great time for fortune to turn the tables on her and grant her wish.

Bits and pieces of her and Colt's discussion after they'd made love flitted through her mind. She'd been up front with him. *There can't be anything other than something casual between us.* Then he'd echoed her sentiments saying they were both adults and could enjoy each other's company. She still saw his smile when he added that there wasn't anything wrong with that. Not exactly the response of a man who wanted a more permanent relationship.

When she'd uttered those words she'd believed them, that she'd be happy with a casual relationship. She wanted more, but couldn't have it. There wasn't a lot of work for an actress in a small Rocky Mountain town of eight thousand people. Plus, her mother was counting on her coming back. How could she bail on her mother with Andrea's marriage on the rocks again?

She'd been a fool to think she could be content with something that paltry. Leaving him was going to be like leaving a part of herself behind. How could she go back to the barren wasteland that had been her life now that she'd seen what life could be like with a true partner to share it with?

She leaned closer to Colt and kissed him. She wanted this one last night to last forever and she wanted that one last time with him. "I think we could leave at ten without causing too much gossip."

Normally Colt enjoyed socializing with his friends and neighbors, but not tonight. By the time he checked his watch for the tenth time since Stacy told him she figured they could leave at ten, he thought he'd go crazy. Nine-forty-five. How could time pass so slowly?

"Quit checking the time. People are going to think you don't want to be here."

He leaned forward to whisper in her ear. "They'd be right because I'd rather be home alone with you."

"Then go on stage. Thank everyone one more time for coming and let's get out of here."

"Yes, ma'am."

He forced himself to stroll up on stage and talk for a full minute before he told everyone to enjoy the rest of the night.

As he and Stacy headed for the front door, he chatted with anyone who stopped him along the way instead of shoving them aside and making a break for the door.

By the time he and Stacy walked into his house five minutes later, his jeans had become more than a bit uncomfortable. No sooner had they walked in the front door than he scooped Stacy into his arms and headed upstairs.

"This is much better than the last time you carried me off."

"You've got to admit you were a pain in the ass then."

"You sure know how to sweet-talk a girl."

He stopped on the stairs and kissed her long and hard, like a man who thought he was drowning and she was the lifeline he'd just latched on to. "I'm a little out of practice."

"You could have fooled me." She slid her hand inside his shirt. Her nails skimmed over his skin sending pleasure bursting through him. He raced up the remaining stairs and into his bedroom.

He tried to swallow the lump in his throat as he placed her on his bed, but the damned thing wouldn't budge. Earlier when Maggie announced the film only had two more days until they wrapped up, he'd wanted to grab Stacy and kiss her until she agreed to stay, because he couldn't bear the thought of her leaving.

Then she'd changed her mind, deciding to stick around for a little longer. He'd gotten a reprieve.

Now he needed to make the most of his time with her.

She held out her arms to him and as he joined her, he forgot everything but her and the pleasure they could find in each other's arms.

Two days later when Maggie called cut, pride over her accomplishment washed over Stacy. Seeing life here through Colt's eyes, becoming a part of Ryan's therapy team had given her insight into her character. Drawing on those things and the connections she now felt to the land and the people around her elevated her performance. No doubt about it, she'd done her best work ever in this movie.

"Filming on *The Women of Spring Creek Ranch* is done! Can you believe it?"

Maggie went on to thank the cast and crew for all their hard work. When everyone started leaving, Maggie approached Stacy and asked to speak to her alone. "The early buzz about the movie is better than I could've ever hoped for. Don't tell anyone, but John Hammond and I are developing a script for a pilot to pitch to the network."

A little flutter raced through Stacy. Hammond had developed more than a few top-rated shows over the years. His latest remained solidly in the top ten ratingswise.

No, she refused to hope. People pitched series all the time and only the tiniest fraction made it to filming a pilot. An even smaller portion got on the air.

"That's wonderful. I know how much it would mean to you to shoot a series here."

"The traveling isn't a problem now because Michaela can come with us, but this is home."

Yes, it was.

"We both know how tough it is to get a series on the air, but I wanted to mention it to you so you could think about it. I can't see anyone else in your role, Stacy. When we get the script done, can I send it to you?"

"Of course."

"Having a bankable star on board would definitely help our pitch with the network."

Maggie's comment shook Stacy. Three months ago she'd struggled to get auditions for A status roles and now she was considered "bankable" enough to impress the network. The entertainment industry could make a girl lightheaded from that quick a climb.

Then the implications of Maggie doing a series sank in and sent thoughts spinning through Stacy's head. A series meant a consistent income. The stability of being in one place, being able to have a predictable home life without worrying about location shoots.

And this series would be shot in Estes Park and eliminate the long-distance relationship factor for her and Colt. Not that he'd given her any indication that he wanted anything more than a casual relationship with her, but that could change in the next few weeks.

Despite knowing she shouldn't hope because that's how she got hurt, Stacy found herself doing just that as she returned to her trailer. Maybe this once fate would cut her a break.

Once inside her trailer, Stacy pulled out her duffel bag to pack up her personal items. She lifted the intricate silver frame containing the picture one of the crew had snapped of her and her father dressed in fifteenth-century finery their first day on the movie set. Her finger traced the surface. What would her father think of Colt? She liked to think he would approve. That he'd say as long as Colt made her happy and was there for her he was pleased. As she placed the photo in her bag, she couldn't help but think how different her life would've been if her father had lived.

Andrea would have someone else to rely on, and I would have had my freedom years ago.

As she packed up her makeup, her cell phone caught her eye. She had three missed calls from her mother and three corresponding voice mails waiting. She massaged the knot in her neck and wondered what her mother wanted now.

She listened to the first message. "Grant doesn't love me. He's having an affair with a young actress. He filed for divorce."

Her mother's voice grew more frantic in the next message. "Why haven't you called me? I need you, Stacy. I always thought you'd be there for me no matter what. That I could count on you."

Stacy's hands shook as she listened to the last message. "I don't know how I can live without Grant. If I'm gone when you get home, please explain things to Ryan."

Gone? She hadn't heard her mother sound that desperate in years. Since Allan, her second husband, left her. Andrea couldn't be thinking of what it sounded like. Her mother wouldn't commit suicide, would she? Her hand trembling, Stacy punched in Andrea's number and prayed she wasn't too late. The phone rang. Once. Twice. Three times before her mother answered.

"Stacy? Why didn't you call sooner?"

"I'm sorry. We were wrapping up filming, and I didn't have my phone with me."

"I can't bear losing Grant." Andrea's voice broke. "I don't do well living alone."

"You'll get through this. It won't be easy, but you can do it."

"I miss your father so much. I want to be with him again." By the time Andrea finished her sentence, her words had started to slur.

"Mom, have you taken something?"

"A couple of Xanax. I'm so tired."

Panic, hot and sharp, bolted through Stacy. "How many did you take?"

"Only a couple."

Buzzing sounded in Stacy's ears. Her mind started to spin. The weight she'd been carrying since her father died crushed her. She started shaking. A chill spread through her as something inside her broke. Maybe if she got cold enough, numb enough, she wouldn't hurt. She didn't want to feel anything because the agony squeezing her heart right now was going to kill her.

"I'm almost positive I didn't take more than a couple."

Andrea's voice pulled Stacy out of her haze. She had to find someone to stay with her mom until she got there. "Don't take any more pills and don't drink any alcohol. I'm going to call Bethany to take you to the hospital and I'll be on the first flight I can get."

"Okay. I can't wait until you come home, Stacy. You'll help me, won't you?"

After she reassured her mother, Stacy called Bethany, Andrea's best friend, who promised she'd get her to the hospital and stay with her until Stacy arrived. Then she booked seats for her and Ryan on the first flight from Denver to L.A., and texted her brother that she was leaving to pick him up at school. Minutes later when he climbed into the car, she updated him on the situation with their mother. "So we're heading home sooner than we planned."

"I should've talked to you about this before now, but I'm not going back."

She struggled to absorb the blows he'd delivered. She wasn't strong enough to fight him right now. Not when she was concerned about her mother. Not when she was being torn apart over having to leave Colt.

"Our mother's on the verge of suicide. If you don't come back it might push her over the edge."

"She won't kill herself. She's too selfish to do that."

"Are you willing to take the risk? I'm not." When he remained stubbornly silent, she said, "We're all the family she has. That's where our home is."

The words rang hollow in her ears. Home? California didn't feel much like home anymore. No, she definitely couldn't call it home anymore.

Because Colt wasn't there.

She couldn't think about that now. If she thought about leaving Colt she'd fall apart.

"That's not where my life is. I'm happy here. I've got more friends, hell, better friends, than I ever had in California." He crossed his arms over his chest, and his hard green eyes flared with teenage defiance. "I'll ask Colt if I could move in with him and Jess. She and I have talked about it. She thinks her dad will be fine with the idea."

"He won't agree to it if I'm not okay with it," she tossed back.

"I'll go to court and get emancipated. Since I'll be eighteen in ten months it shouldn't be a big deal."

"Why are you doing this?" She loved him so much and had practically raised him. Couldn't Ryan see how he was destroying her?

"Why are you rushing back to her? What's she ever done for us other than give birth to us?"

"She's our mother. We're family and sometimes being part of a family requires making sacrifices."

"But we're always the ones doing the sacrificing." He stared out the window. Though he sat beside her in the passenger seat, he felt so far away. "I'll do whatever I have to so I can stay here. I have the right to be happy. I won't go back."

For the majority of Ryan's life she'd told herself she'd wanted her brother to have choices she never had, but now that he could choose to stay in Estes Park when she couldn't, jealousy mixed with white-hot anger tore her apart. Granted Andrea wouldn't ever win parent of the year, but didn't they both owe her something? They couldn't leave her to fall apart.

Stacy didn't have time for a knock-down, drag-out fight with him, especially one she wasn't strong enough to survive. Ryan had to go back to California with her because she couldn't cope with Andrea and her problems alone. She needed someone to listen, someone who understood what she was going through, someone to hold her together, but how could she convince Ryan?

She probably couldn't, but Colt could. She pulled into the nearest parking lot, turned around and headed for Colt's ranch. "We'll see what Colt has to say about this."

"I'm coming. Hold on," Colt called out as he made his way to the front door. "Quit ringing the blasted doorbell. You're giving me a headache."

He yanked open the door and found Stacy standing there, her face drawn, her arms crossed over her chest, fire blazing in her eyes. "You've got to talk to Ryan. My mom's threatening to commit suicide, and he's in the car refusing to go back to California with me. He thinks he can move in here with you and Jess. Tell him he can't live here."

His head spun from the verbal assault she'd just hurled at him. Her mother threatened to commit suicide? What the hell had happened? Then add Ryan with his teenage dander up and no wonder she was spitting mad. Considering their moods, he bet neither one of them was listening to the other. It's a wonder they arrived at the ranch in one piece. He walked past Stacy, strode over to the car and rapped on the passenger window.

Ryan rolled down the window. Attitude and teenage defiance rolled off him in waves. "What?"

"Join Jess in the kitchen."

When the teenager opened his mouth, Colt shook his head. "Don't say anything. We'll work this out, but you and your sister need to calm down first."

Ryan got out of the car, slammed the door hard enough to make Colt's teeth rattle and stormed up to the house. He clomped past his sister leaning on his cane without even looking in her direction.

"Wait a minute. Come back here," Stacy yelled at her brother.

"Let him go."

Stacy clutched his arms. Her nails dug into his skin. "Tell him he can't move in here. Tell him it's his duty to come with me."

"We need to talk first. Tell me what happened."

She told him about her mother's voice mails and their conversation. The more he listened, the angrier he became at her mother. Lord. What kind of woman leaves a message for her daughter saying she's going to commit suicide and blames it on her child for not "being there" for her? The woman could teach Catholic nuns a thing or two about imposing guilt on others.

Knowing his anger wouldn't help Stacy, he stuffed the emotion down. Though he wanted to scoop her into his arms, hold her and tell her everything would be all right, he knew that wasn't what she needed right now, either. She was wound too tight and holding on by a thread. Her gaze held the same glazed and frenzied look he'd seen in green soldiers' eyes the first time they came under fire.

Remaining factual and detached was the best way to go. That and helping her sort through what to do. So instead of holding her, he clasped her hand and led her into the living room where he settled onto the couch and patted the spot beside him. She shook her head, refusing to sit and started pacing instead.

"I'm so tired of holding what little family I have together. When my dad died, my mother crawled into a hole. Ryan was so little then. On the nanny's day off Andrea let him cry in his crib. I was the one who went to him. Later, I was the one he ran to when he fell down. Not our mother. She was too busy trying to snag a husband or keep one the one she'd caught."

"You raised him."

"That's why his wanting to stay here hurts so bad. I can't lose him. He's all I have."

You have me. The words almost jumped out, but now wasn't the time to talk about how he felt. She had enough to think about with Ryan and her mom. He refused to add to her emotional turmoil. "This isn't what you want to hear, but you can't force Ryan to go back to California."

Her expressive face tightened with anger as she circled his living room. "You're right. I don't want to hear that."

"I won't lie to you to make you feel better because that won't do you any good. If you push him too hard you risk making him even more determined. He'll do the opposite of what you want just to prove you can't force him to do anything. That's where you're headed by playing this game of chicken. I found that out the hard way. I almost lost Jess when I went to Afghanistan."

"Really?"

She sank onto the couch beside him. He told her how he'd missed the signs Jess sent out about needing him around more. He hadn't wanted to see them because he knew if he did he'd have to make changes in his life. He'd have to give up the career he loved. Then he explained about the troubles Reed and Jess had while he was in Afghanistan and how Jess ran away. "I learned something else while I was gone. Teenagers aren't really kids anymore."

"That may be true, but they're not old enough to make their own decisions, either. Ryan has to go back with me. He's not old enough to be on his own."

"Right now you don't have a choice. You can't make him go with you, and you don't have time to convince him. Focus on your mother and getting her help. Let Ryan stay here with me and Jess."

"I don't know if I can bear letting him go."

"You've basically been Ryan's parent. Part of taking on that job means sucking it up and taking a hit because you want what's best for your child."

"Like you gave up your military career."

He nodded.

"My mother never learned that lesson. I always said I'd never make the mistakes she did." Her eyes filled with tears. "I have to let him go, don't I?"

Colt nodded and wrapped his arms around her. He held her for a minute while she cried. Then when she'd gotten everything out of her system, together they walked into the kitchen and he stood beside her as she told her brother she was leaving for California, but he could stay.

Ryan turned to his sister, his eyes wide. "You're letting me live here with Colt and Jess? Permanently?"

Stacy bit her lip and nodded. She was trying so hard to hold it together. "I want you to be happy."

"Thanks." Ryan strode across the room and wrapped his sister in a big hug. "When do you think you'll be back?"

The reality of her leaving and that she might not return hit Colt head-on. The ache, the pain coursing through him threatened to bring him to his knees. He held his breath and his palms grew sweaty as he waited for her to answer Ryan's question.

The silence stretched. That wasn't a good sign and he knew it.

What had he expected her to do? Say she couldn't wait to come back? That she'd give up her life, her career to see if they could make a go of being a family?

"I don't know. It'll depend on how Mom does. I start shooting my next movie in six weeks, but if she goes into a mental hospital, who knows how long it'll be before I can leave her." She turned in Colt's direction, but she failed to meet his gaze as she nibbled on her lower lip. "Thank you for taking Ryan in. I'll call to discuss the legal issues and support payments."

The last bit of his hope that her going was only temporary, that she'd say she couldn't leave him for good, that she loved him and wanted him in her life withered and died. What she'd just said made it clear that she wasn't coming back any time soon.

"I don't need your money."

I need you. The words hovered in his mind, but he shoved them aside. If she'd give him a sliver of hope, maybe he could tell her how he felt. He could ask her to come back to him when her mother was better, but only an idiot spilled his guts to a woman after she gave him a giant "it's over" signal like Stacy just had.

"I know, but I'm going to help with his support anyway."

He peered into her beautiful blue eyes. He thought Lynn leaving him hurt. That was nothing compared to what he felt now. Lynn had been the love of his youth. Stacy was the love of his life. "When's your flight?"

"Nine-twenty tonight."

He nodded, not sure what to say or do. Should he smile at the woman he loved, say things were fun while they lasted and ask if they could keep in touch via Skype or Facebook?

He wanted her in his life forever, but their lives were so different. He couldn't move to California. He thought about how unhappy Lynn had been when she'd given up her dreams of living in the city for him. He wouldn't make that mistake with a woman again. He loved Stacy, but he had to let her go.

She nodded, as well. Then she walked across the room, kissed him on the cheek and walked out the door.

At least if Ryan moved in with him and Jess maybe he'd see Stacy when she visited her brother. Would having her in his life that way be better or worse than not having a relationship with her? Talk about exquisite torture, and how pathetic was he to consider being willing to accept that?

The deafening sound of the door closing behind her echoed through his silent house.

"Why are you letting her go?" Jess swatted him on the arm. "Do something."

He'd had all he could take. "I'm not discussing this." He turned to Ryan. "We need to get your things."

Then Colt headed for the door as well, the teenager trailing after him. When they reached his driveway, Stacy's car was nowhere in sight. His heart sank. Had he really expected her to be sitting in her car waiting to tell him she'd changed her mind?

After a couple of minutes of awkward silence on the road, Ryan said, "I know you said you didn't want to talk, but you care about my sister. What I don't get is why you're letting her go back to California."

"Give a guy a heads-up before you toss out a bomb like that, especially when he's driving."

"You're avoiding my question."

Damn straight. "I didn't *let* Stacy do anything. Weren't you listening to the conversations she had with you today? She's got a mind of her own, and she made it clear to both of us that her life's in California. Now change the subject."

"There are some things you need to know about my sister, so I'm going to talk, and you're going to listen."

Colt thought about arguing with Ryan, but truth be told he didn't have the strength. It would be easier to tune the kid out.

"Stacy's always been too nice, and our mother's used that and her mind games to keep Stacy under her thumb. Without Stacy, our mom would have to take care of herself. She would have to get a job if Stacy quit bailing her out financially."

"She supports your mom?"

Ryan nodded. "I don't know about right after Dad died because I was a baby, but I do know about the past few years. Mom loves the Hollywood lifestyle. She spends her days working with her personal trainer, shopping and having three-hour lunches with her friends at four-star restaurants." Ryan told Colt how Andrea lost a good part of the money her first husband left her in a divorce settlement with her second. "Stacy hasn't had much luck getting our mother to live within her means, and she can't say no when Mom comes up short."

Life had forced Stacy to grow up as fast as

he had. They'd both had parents who bailed on them. Ones who couldn't cope with life. Colt's father crawled into a bottle and lashed out with his fists. Stacy's mom tried to fill the void with men and a lavish lifestyle.

"Did you ask Stacy to stay?" Ryan asked.

"Not outright, but I hinted at it."

"What did you say? Something like if you want to, you could stay here for a while?"

Pretty much, and hearing Ryan parrot basically what he'd said to Stacy didn't make the words sound any better than when he'd originally uttered them. What woman would take a man up on a botched invitation like that?

"What if she's waiting for you to say you *want* her to stay?"

One thing he admired about Stacy was how she spoke her mind. He never had to guess with her, and since he'd known her, she'd been clear that her career and her life were in California.

"Your sister's not a beat-around-the-bush kind of gal."

"But she's not big on asking for stuff for herself because people always expect her to be strong. Andrea once told her she never had to worry about her because she'll always be all right."

Colt shook his head. "Your mom's a piece of work."

"That's what I've been trying to tell Stacy. When I was younger I used to ask our mom to do things with me, read to me or take me places. She always had an excuse why she couldn't. She was busy. She couldn't leave her husband alone for us to go somewhere for the day. Whatever. I learned to ask Stacy instead. She always had time for me. Growing up Stacy didn't have anyone else to turn to. I think the way she coped was she learned to quit asking."

Life with a father who responded to requests for help with a quick fist and criticism taught Colt to be self-sufficient. What if Stacy learned a similar lesson? What had Ryan just said? Stacy learned to quit asking. What if they'd both been sitting back waiting for the other to open up? Were he and Stacy two people who'd been so overlooked by their families that they'd grown afraid to reach out to anyone for fear they'd end up getting knocked down?

Colt pulled up to the cabin where Ryan and his sister had been staying. If he never told Stacy he loved her and asked her to be part of his life, he'd always wonder what she would've said. Sure it was a risk and he could get hurt if she rejected him, but what if she said yes?

The biggest rewards often required the biggest risk. "Since you're here talking to me like this, I'm guessing you approve of me seeing your sister?"

"That question's so stupid I'm not going to answer it."

He had Ryan's blessing, now he needed his daughter's.

An hour later when Colt and Ryan returned to the house, Ryan went upstairs to settle into the guest room while Colt asked Jess to join him in the living room. He couldn't ask Stacy to be a part of his life unless his daughter supported his decision. When they'd placed the squalling wrinkled pink bundle in his arms almost sixteen years ago, he'd entered into a lifelong commitment.

He'd screwed up when he'd learned of his deployment by not laying everything out with Jess. He'd talked to her, but they never really had a heart-to-heart, compromise and work it out discussion. He may not be Albert Einstein, but he was smart enough to learn from his mistakes. He knew that, but he wasn't quite sure how to start. "I'm sorry I snapped at you earlier."

"That's not what you want to talk to me about. I know something's up because you're acting like you do whenever you've got something to discuss that you don't want to talk about."

"How did you get to be so smart?"

"Good genes." She grinned, looking so much like her mother. He and Lynn may have failed at marriage, but they'd created something incredible in this amazing young woman.

"I'm in love with Stacy."

"I know. You have that same look in your eyes that Uncle Reed does when he looks at Avery. The question is what are you going to do about it?"

His daughter's words nearly knocked him over. She'd grown up so fast. He'd been right when he told Stacy earlier that teenagers really weren't kids anymore. "I want to ask her to marry me, but before I do, I want to make sure you're okay with it."

"What if I said I'm not?"

"Then I wouldn't ask her to marry me, but I won't stop seeing her." He searched his daughter's young face, trying to read her thoughts and then decided to quit guessing. "Are you saying you're not okay with it?"

"She's cool. I like how she makes you

happy." Jess's brows furrowed in thought. He braced himself. Experience taught him her looking like that or thinking that hard never led to something he wanted to hear. "What will that make Ryan? My stepuncle? That borders on creepy."

"You may not have to worry about that. Stacy may turn me down."

His daughter laughed until her eyes watered. "Really, Dad? Come on. The woman ran into a burning barn to save you."

Maybe there was hope for him.

Stacy sat in the unforgiving plastic chairs connected like train cars in the Denver airport and realized she'd made the biggest mistake of her life.

She was leaving behind everyone who filled her life with light. Ryan, Jess and, most importantly, Colt. She'd finally found a man she wanted to share her life with, one who'd stood beside her, one who hadn't bailed on her when she needed him or told her she was more trouble than she was worth, and what was she doing? Walking away from him, and for what? A needy, self-centered mother and a career that made a roller-coaster ride look like a smooth experience.

Hardly a fair trade.

Nannette's words hammered in Stacy's mind. *You're not your mother's keeper. You have the right to live your own life.*

As a child she'd lacked the power to do anything about Andrea relying on her as a confidant and a source of financial support. At some point that was no longer true. Since then, by allowing the unhealthy patterns she and Andrea had settled into to continue, Stacy had become part of the problem.

But no more.

She refused to sacrifice her life for her mother any longer. She'd tell Andrea she'd always be there for her, but she wouldn't continue to rescue her. Stacy vowed she'd get her through this rough time with Grant, but then her mother was going to have to learn to stand on her own two feet, to call her own repairmen and live within her own means.

I deserve that.

Nannette had been right. Everyone's life was tough. The giant weight that had been resting on Stacy's chest tumbled off.

Colt had shown her what life could be like, and she intended to do whatever she could to hold on to that. Nothing in her life meant anything if she wasn't with him.

She couldn't leave with things unsettled between them, without telling him how much she loved him. She wanted him in her life. However she could have him. Her hand shaking, she clutched her cell phone and called the man she loved.

When he answered, she plunged forward before she lost her courage. She stared at the floor as she struggled to control her racing thoughts. "I should have said this earlier, but I was afraid to. I'd like us to keep seeing each other even though I'm moving back to California. Once I help my mom through this latest crisis then I can think about the future. I know this is a lot to ask of you because I travel so much for my job and long-distance relationships are hard. I know this isn't the kind of thing people usually discuss over the phone, but—"

"I want to talk about it, too, but do you mind if I sit down?"

Worn, scuffed cowboy boots materialized in her line of vision and her heart nearly jumped out of her chest. They looked like Colt's, but weren't men in Colorado required by law to own a pair of dog-eared cowboy boots? Her gaze traveled upward until she reached his magnificent face.

This couldn't be real. She was missing him so much she'd started hallucinating. "Am I seeing things or are you really here?"

He shoved his cell phone in his back pocket and then pried hers out of her hand, ended the call and dropped it in her purse. "I'm here. I want to correct a mistake I made earlier." He folded his long muscular frame into the plastic seat beside her. "I never should've let you leave. I love you."

Joy, full and overpowering, exploded inside her. "Only ticketed passengers are allowed at the gate."

A bewildered look crossed his handsome features. "Not exactly the response I expected after my declaration of love."

Finally coming out of her fog, she said, "I love you, too."

His warm, callused hands cupped her face. He felt real. Solid. Tears filled her eyes as he lightly kissed her. Then he slid out of his chair, the plastic scrunching and creaking with his movement, and he knelt in front of her. "You're the best thing that's ever happened to me. Other than with Jess and my brother, I haven't had a lot of luck with family. My father was an abusive bastard who drank himself into an early grave. My mother died when I was twelve, and you know about my marriage, but Stacy, I love you with all my heart. Marry me."

"Yes, I'll marry you."

Colt stood, scooped her into his arms and swung her around as he let out a whoop of joy. Applause erupted around them. She blushed, noticing that they'd drawn a crowd.

"But how do we make things work, practically speaking? I don't know how to do anything but act. Sure, Griffin and Maggie are keeping their careers going, but she's a director and has more control over the projects she does than I do."

"If you can put the breaks on the train you've got barreling down the tracks we can talk about it."

"When I get super nervous I tend to talk a lot."

"I noticed." He set her back on the floor and his knuckles brushed her cheek. "We won't starve if you don't work."

"I won't let you support me."

"I'll do whatever I have to for you to be a part of my life. If that means you going where you need to in order to film a movie, then that's what we'll do, and I'll be here waiting for you. I'll console myself with thinking about how good getting back together will be."

"You'd do that for me?"

"We'll work it out because we're family."

The realization that that's what she, Colt,

Ryan and Jess were rippled through her, filling all the empty spots in her heart. She finally had what she'd always longed for. "We are, aren't we?" She smiled, but then asked, "Wait a minute. You never answered my question about what you're doing here at the gate."

He reached into his back pocket, pulled out a boarding pass and held the paper out to her. Los Angeles. Her flight number. She read the information twice, but still refused to believe it. "You're coming to L.A.?"

"You said you couldn't cope with your mother's problems on your own. We'll handle the situation together, and then I'm making sure you come back home with me."

Back home. She liked the sound of that.

* * * * *

HOME on the RANCH

YES! Please send me the **Home on the Ranch Collection** in Larger Print. This collection begins with 3 FREE books and 2 FREE gifts in the first shipment. Along with my 3 free books, I'll also get the next 4 books from the Home on the Ranch Collection, in LARGER PRINT, which I may either return and owe nothing, or keep for the low price of $5.24 U.S./ $5.89 CDN each plus $2.99 for shipping and handling per shipment*. If I decide to continue, about once a month for 8 months I will get 6 or 7 more books, but will only need to pay for 4. That means 2 or 3 books in every shipment will be FREE! If I decide to keep the entire collection, I'll have paid for only 32 books because 19 books are FREE! I understand that accepting the 3 free books and gifts places me under no obligation to buy anything. I can always return a shipment and cancel at any time. My free books and gifts are mine to keep no matter what I decide.

268 HCN 3760 468 HCN 3760

Name	(PLEASE PRINT)	
Address		Apt. #
City	State/Prov.	Zip/Postal Code

Signature (if under 18, a parent or guardian must sign)

Mail to the **Reader Service**:

IN U.S.A.: P.O. Box 1341, Buffalo, New York 14240-8531
IN CANADA: P.O. Box 603, Fort Erie, Ontario L2A 5X3

* Terms and prices subject to change without notice. Prices do not include applicable taxes. Sales tax applicable in NY. Canadian residents will be charged applicable taxes. This offer is limited to one order per household. All orders subject to approval. Credit or debit balances in a customer's account(s) may be offset by any other outstanding balance owed by or to the customer. Please allow 3 to 4 weeks for delivery. Offer available while quantities last. Offer not available to Quebec residents.

HRCBPA18R

Get 4 FREE REWARDS!

We'll send you 2 FREE Books plus 2 FREE Mystery Gifts.

FREE Value Over **$20**

Both the **Romance** and **Suspense** collections feature compelling novels written by many of today's best-selling authors.

YES! Please send me 2 FREE novels from the Essential Romance or Essential Suspense Collection and my 2 FREE gifts (gifts are worth about $10 retail). After receiving them, if I don't wish to receive any more books, I can return the shipping statement marked "cancel." If I don't cancel, I will receive 4 brand-new novels every month and be billed just $6.74 each in the U.S. or $7.24 each in Canada. That's a savings of at least 16% off the cover price. It's quite a bargain! Shipping and handling is just 50¢ per book in the U.S. and 75¢ per book in Canada*. I understand that accepting the 2 free books and gifts places me under no obligation to buy anything. I can always return a shipment and cancel at any time. The free books and gifts are mine to keep no matter what I decide.

Choose one: ☐ **Essential Romance** (194/394 MDN GMY7)   ☐ **Essential Suspense** (191/391 MDN GMY7)

STRS18

Name (please print)

Address   Apt. #

City   State/Province   Zip/Postal Code

Mail to the **Reader Service:**
IN U.S.A.: P.O. Box 1341, Buffalo, NY 14240-8531
IN CANADA: P.O. Box 603, Fort Erie, Ontario L2A 5X3

Want to try two free books from another series? Call 1-800-873-8635 or visit www.ReaderService.com.